BECK AND CALL

Beck and Call

HANNA WALDON

Alex Zandrea Books

To everyone who believes in the power of second chances.

Spotify Playlist

Hold Me While You Wait - Lewis Capaldi
Easy On Me - Adele
Why Am I Waiting - Papithbk
Teenage Dirtbag - Wheetus
Perfect - Ed Sheeran
Still Falling For You - Ellie Goulding
That Way - Tate McRae
If You Love Her - Forest Blakk
I Didn't Know - Sofia Carson
Only You - Ellie Goulding

Chapter 1

Lydia

I got the house.

I hadn't really wondered whether or not I would get it, but it seems to be all that I can think about now. That I had gotten the house in the divorce. There wasn't much opposition on Tristan's part, truthfully. When the judge in the municipal court had told us that I would be allowed to keep our house and all of the belongings, all he did was sigh dejectedly and slump down in his chair a bit, as though he'd had his order messed up at a restaurant. But still, I had gotten the house, and at the time, it felt like a win.

I got the house. And now, standing in the entryway alone, I wish that I hadn't.

The loneliness is almost palpable. I don't wish that Tristan was here, of course, but it's far larger and more quiet than I remembered it being. I thought that it would be nice to be just me, free to do what I wanted without having to hear his opinions of everything that I was doing.

Instead, it feels like the emptiness is threatening to swallow me whole.

I stand there in the doorway for an undetermined amount of time before I finally find the courage to walk inside and face the destitution.

The first thing that I notice is how clean everything is. How quiet and still it is. The silence hangs in the air like a fog, impossible to ignore. Has it always been like this?

No, it hasn't. Probably it had been for the last few months, since Tristan had moved out, but I had been so preoccupied with the divorce proceedings piling up on top of my own work that I'd retreated inside myself, incapable of noticing my surroundings. Now, they face me head-on and unrelenting, and I am suffocated.

Suddenly, my clothes feel too tight.

It's all I can do not to scream. Every inch of the fabric of my satin blouse feels like a straightjacket, my jeans feel like they're made of sandpaper against my skin, and I can hardly breathe as I drop my work bags to the floor with a thud. I need to get out of these clothes. The hot itch of hives that are slowly creeping up my chest to my neck are doing nothing to help matters, adding to the panic and the overwhelm of this great alone.

I power walk my way towards my bedroom, kicking my wedges off in the hallway and practically throwing my belt into the living room as I go. My jeans are next, and I nearly topple over as I shove them down my waist and to the ground, tripping over myself. Then, my blouse. I think I hear a stitch pop as I pull the thing over my head, getting a bit tangled up in the process. In my haste, I neglected to unbutton it, making it tighter than it should be and threatening to send me over the edge at any second.

"Shit," I swear, shimmying and twisting my arms into knots as I try to free myself from it, feeling my breathing growing more ragged by the second. Trapped. I'm trapped. I thought I got out, thought the divorce was going to free me, but I'm still trapped. Trapped in this house, trapped in this stupid shirt, trapped in my own head—

My self-deprecation spiral is interrupted by the sound of my phone ringing on the floor.

The generic ringtone jolts me back to reality. Finally free from the clutches of The Shirt, I huff out a sigh, bending over to pick it up and swiping to answer without missing a beat.

"Lydia Michaelson, Henry Brothers Law Firm, how may I help you?"

"Um, Dee? Why are you shirtless?" Olivia's voice rings through the phone, and I freeze. I'd been dreading the very real possibility that this could be one of those work calls that you end up having to stay on for a full hour and a half after you've already gotten home from your regular shift that makes you question your sanity.

Instead, it's so much worse.

I hadn't even realized that I had been answering Face-Time when I picked up the phone. Now, I'm met with the image of my older sister's shocked expression, clearly on a crowded street. My face heats.

"Oh my God," I stammer out, dropping my phone onto my bed as I scramble to find something, anything to pull on over my head so that I'm not showing my breasts to the general public via my sister's iPhone. The first thing I grab is the (now far too small) Texas Pete's Hot Sauce t-shirt that I've been sleeping in since high school. I pull it on, neglecting to check to see if it was even right side out (surprise, it wasn't) before I grab my phone again, pushing my wild curls out of my face. "Jesus, I'm so sorry. Please tell me no one saw that."

"Actually, I tapped the shoulder of the strange man in front of me and got him to turn around to look at the screen by saying 'Hey, check out my sister's tits! Free semi-nudity!'"

"Shut up."

"No one saw, Dee." I heave a sigh of relief. Collapsing onto my bed, I rub my eyes with the heel of my hand, mascara be damned.

"I think I'm losing my mind," I say, and Olivia shrugs.

"If you weren't, I would be more worried. You just went through a divorce. A life-altering event. Acknowledging the fact that it's hard is the first step towards healing."

"Since when did you become my therapist?"

"Don't give me that title. I'm not stable enough to hear even half of the things you've told Noelle. Too empathetic. I would just start crying and ruin it for both of us."

"Right."

"Did you want to know the reason I called you?" My sister says, and I notice the mischievous grin on her face coming across the screen. My brow furrows.

"I was getting there, but now you're scaring me. Why are you smiling like that?"

"Like what?"

"Like you're secretly a serial murderer."

"Oh, come on." Olivia scoffs, and the screen drops from her face momentarily. The jingle of keys and the creak of door hinges are all I can hear for a moment as she steps into her apartment. We're both quiet for a moment, and then she plops down on the couch, a less disconcerting smile having replaced the previously deranged look on her face.

"So get on with it. Why'd you call?" I ask, sitting up in bed a little, curious.

"Did you get a package today?" She asks, and I shake my head. "Let me rephrase that. Did you check to see if you'd gotten a package today?" When I shake my head again, she gives me a knowing glance.

"I was a little..." Depressed? Lonely? Contemplating the merits of cutting my own bangs in the mirror to see if the change makes me feel something other than numb? "I was preoccupied."

"I think you should check." I let out a small huff, and begrudgingly, I stand. Surely enough, when I look out on my porch, there's a package that I had neglected to notice sitting on my front porch.

"Okay, I did get one," I say, swiping out of FaceTime momentarily as I pick up the package, balancing my phone on top of it so that I can awkwardly maneuver myself back through my doorway. "It's heavier than it looks. I mean, God, what's in this, Liv? Rocks?"

"Just open it already," she pleads, and I almost scold her for being whiny. I let out a little sound of assent as I hoist the box onto the kitchen counter. Pausing for a second, I read the company name on the shipping label: Wine Not Celebrate. I don't give myself time to criticize the company's name, as badly as I want to, because I don't want to make Olivia feel bad. I grab a butter knife out of one of the drawers and get to work opening the box; Inside is an abundance of bright pink packing material and a wooden crate with a little gold latch on the side. I open it to reveal an equally pink interior, with a bottle of Rosé on the inside. A bottle of Rosé with a custom label.

In bold letters, it reads: Pairs Well with Freshly-Signed Divorce Papers.

The laugh that bubbles up out of my throat is nearly humorless. I feel tears stinging at the backs of my eyes, coming on in a wave of emotion that I can't fight back, can't tamp down. When I finally turn my attention back to my phone to see the way my sister is gauging my reaction, I watch her face shift from anticipation to mild panic.

"Oh my God, Dee. Oh God, I'm so sorry, my timing is horrible. We got them for a work party at Small & Sparkling and I thought it would be funny. I thought—"

"It is funny! I'm laughing, right? I promise it's funny," I insist, even though my laughter has quickly devolved into sobbing. "I'm fine, Olivia. I'm fine. I promise."

And even as I insist this, I'm wiping my eyes with the backs of my arm, trying to focus on taking deep breaths. In and out. In and out.

It's another long moment before either of us say anything. I can tell that Olivia doesn't want to leave me alone like this, no matter how awkward it's making her feel to watch me sobbing over a slightly grainy video call. Once I finally get my breathing under control, I smile

at her, picking up the bottle of wine and examining it a bit closer. It looks to be a dry Rosé, the kind I like best on a hot summer day, and I nod approvingly in the direction of my phone.

"You chose perfectly," I say, glad that she took the time to remember my preferences.

"Thank you. I mean it."

"Of course," She nods, offering me a sad smile. "Hey, if you need me, I'm here. You know that, right?" My sister sounds deeply sincere, her voice colored with an air of concern. "It's important to me that you know that."

"I do know," I nod. "I promise I know." And I mean it. I would do anything for my sister, and I know that same sentiment extends to me.

"Should I let you go?"

"Probably, yeah," I offer her a laugh that's halfway between a genuine chuckle and a self-pitying one. "I want to pop open this bottle and drown my sorrows."

"Okay, but you have to promise me one thing."

"What's that?"

"No Legally Blonde. And no Adele. He doesn't deserve that level of sadness from you."

This time, my laugh is more genuine. She knows me too well.

"That's two things."

"Lydia."

"Okay. I love you."

"Love you."

The line goes dead and the place where my sister's face had been is replaced by my bleak home screen. I sigh, taking in the pristine surroundings of my kitchen and the meticulously placed decorations. I remember how desperately I longed for it to look parisian when we had

first moved in, but not in the way that a 12-year-old girl might want her bedroom to look "parisian". I had coordinated the exposed brick backsplash with the multicolored planter box in the windowsill and the gold hanging basket that I kept stocked with fresh fruit. There were paintings of bicycles on town streets and floral valances on my windows that let in the perfect amount of sun and the kitchen island doubled as a bar cart. There wasn't any shortage of decorations because my worst fear had been my house looking too plain or white or sterile. It was beautiful.

But, all at once, I was struck by the realization that it didn't look like anyone actually lived here. Like it was a house that had been curated for a magazine or for photoshoots. There weren't any signs of life.

Maybe because I hadn't necessarily felt alive here in quite some time.

I'd lost count of all of the impulsive cleaning I had done over the past few months. I took

"controlling what you can" to a level that I hadn't even noticed when I had started.

My home has become soulless. And I desperately need a way out.

Chapter 2

Beck

If I'm being honest with myself, I know that my job is nothing but a means to an end. Never once have I claimed to be passionate about the stock market or investing, but I'd had to decide on a major when I got to college, and all of the other guys in my frat had chosen business. Or engineering. But the thought of doing math for the rest of my life made me want to crawl in a hole, so I picked business. At least that way, I could be in classes with my friends, I reasoned. The next thing I knew, I was in a job at a financial advising firm that I had no idea how I'd found myself in, caring immensely about bottom lines and market trends and teetering on losing my mind.

Then, I lost my wife. We'd been married for under a year when she got in the accident.

So, in what I now know to be a quarter-life crisis, I started trying out hobbies.

This is the kind of thing that happens when you are grieving. It might not be an obvious coping mechanism to everyone, but as my therapist likes to say, everyone grieves differently, so it's perfectly normal to want to find purpose when the one thing you actually found purpose in leaves you too soon. First, it was mountain biking. I gave that up after the first time I fell and nearly sent myself careening down a steep cliff face, promptly deciding that thrill-seeking ventures likely weren't going to be for me. Then, I tried chess, but upon attending my first session at a local chess club, realized how much actual studying and pattern memorization that people do to understand and consequently become good at chess (it wasn't anything like The Queen's Gambit).

Finally, when I was just about to give up hope and resign myself to a life of misery at a desk job, fueled by nights out and giving myself over to the scene of meaningless alcohol-fueled

hookups, I found pottery. It started with my sister. She'd brought me with her to some mug painting and wine event that her yoga studio was hosting, because she said it would be "good for me to get out". The place had doubled as the owner's personal studio, and I was immediately and immensely fascinated by the mechanics of the pottery wheel. The way that he was able to create something out of nothing, shape and form being made out of what had just been, essentially, a clump of wet dirt. (When I say it this way to people with an actual art background, they generally scoff or laugh or some combination of the two things.)

Even still, though, I've learned to love the creative process, and have pretty much taught myself how to make vases and bowls and various other sculptures over the past two years, finding meaning in the mess. And now, every Wednesday after work, I get to look forward to going to a pottery studio downtown so that I can practice and hone my craft.

So, when my sister had called me one Wednesday a few months ago, I nearly ignored it, trying to focus on what was in front of me on the wheel. But when I spared a glance down at my phone, there were at least eight text messages, and they were written in all caps, which I know

Amber only uses when she's excited.

From: Amber (sis)
BECK
BECKSTER
BECK ANSWER THE PHONE
PLEASE
I KNOW YOU'RE AT POTTERY
CLASS
BUT THIS IS HUGE
LYDIA IS FINALLY LOSING
THE LOSER

TELLING THE LOSER TO

GET LOST, IF YOU WILL
PICK UPPPPPPPPP

My brain whirred about a thousand miles a minute. I didn't know what it meant — I knew that Lydia's marriage to Tristan was rocky, and I knew that Amber knew how I felt about Lydia back in high school.

Then, my phone started to ring again, and I wiped the clay off of my hands onto my apron. I answered quickly, maybe a little too quickly.

"Glad I could get your attention, Picasso," My sister chirped, and I let out a huff.

"Picasso was a painter—"

"Not the point. Did you get my texts?"

"I did."

"Lydia's getting a divorce!" She said it like someone had won the lottery, and that said person was me. I took in a sharp breath. I don't remember how exactly I felt in that moment, but I do remember at the very least being relieved. Tristan had been an asshole, a drunk, someone we all hated — and had been the reason that Lydia and I hadn't seen each other in nearly three years.

"Wow," Was all I could manage.

"Wow? That's it? That's all you have to say about your best friend and your nearly debilitating high school crush finally being single again after, what, nearly a decade?"

"Amber, it's not that simple. Of course, I'm glad she's finally coming to her senses about that asshole, of course I am, but it just—"

"I'm not suggesting you do anything about it, dummy. It's way too soon for that." She said, voice nearly scolding, and I mentally chastised myself for even thinking that it had been her intention. Of course it wasn't.

It had been my instinct to react to this in a more visceral way. To try and force romance out of something with Lydia.

At that moment, I had the realization that nothing had really changed. That my heart really was still hers, even after all these years. Even after Heather.

Heather. Heather. Just thinking about her at the same time as Lydia filled me with some irrational and unshakeable guilt. It had been over two years by that point, and I had done plenty of healing.

But apparently, based on the pang in my chest, I wasn't necessarily ready to think about

that either.

It had been silent for far too long on my end before I finally tuned back into the conversation.

"Hellooooo? Earth to Beck?" My sister asked in a sing-songy voice, "You there, or did I lose you?"

"I'm here, sorry. Just..."

"Lost in thought?"

"Yeah."

"Heather?" Amber sounded sad when she said her name, and I knew that the sadness wasn't just for me. It was her own sadness, too.

"Yeah," I said again, clearing my throat. "Just..."

"You don't have to explain."

"Thank you," I muttered, willing myself not to break down, finding myself laser-focused again on the small and currently incomplete vase on the wheel in front of me. "I'm gonna go, though. Get back to it."

"Alright, Da Vinci, just—"

"Again, Da Vinci was a painter."

"Whatever. Can I just tell you one last thing?"

"Go ahead." A beat passed, and I imagined my sister gearing herself up to say whatever it was that she was about to. Steeling herself.

"When... when you are ready, and when Lydia is ready, I know that... I know that

Heather would have wanted you to go for it. That she would want you to be happy."

I should have known this was coming. I'd heard it before, in therapy sessions and at my grief support group meetings. Logically, I knew that it was true. That Heather wouldn't want me to wallow in my misery and let myself do nothing but miss her forever. That she would likely make some joke about how I was "wasting my hotness" by not using it, that I was "doing humanity a disservice" or something of the sort.

Still, I couldn't get myself to believe it.

"Thanks," I managed, a tight smile on my face that I hoped she couldn't somehow sense.

"I gotta go. Talk to you soon."

"Alright. Bye, bud."

"See ya."

For the rest of class, Lydia was all I could think about.

***

I didn't forget that conversation. But, when I get a notification on my phone from Lydia's contact, I'm still surprised. I had resigned myself not to reach out until she reached out to me. Even though we'd been best friends once, had grown up together and spent nearly every summer together since we were kids on vacation with our families, it still feels... feels unreal seeing her

name pop up on my screen after so many years of short conversations to wish one another Happy Birthday or the occasional holiday greeting here and there. Immediately, I feel it again — that strange cocktail of sorrow and guilt and longing.

All of a sudden, I feel the need to steel myself to open the text. I stand up from the spot on my brown leather couch that Amber teasingly calls my "bachelor furniture" and cross my apartment to my liquor cabinet, pouring myself a double scotch, neat. I throw the liquid back, relishing the warmth and the sting in my throat, and pushing my (probably too long) blonde waves back out of my face like I'm actually about to see her. I'm giddy and nervous and it's only over a text.

Another sip of the liquor, and then, I finally swipe my phone open to my texts.

From: Lydia M.
Hey.

I almost double over, laughing in spite of myself and partially at myself. I don't know what I had been expecting — anything other than a casual greeting like this would have been almost absurd. I slump back down on my couch as I type out a reply.

Hi. Been a minute.

A few moments pass. I decide to turn on my TV to have something to distract myself with. Equally, I figure it might not be best to respond immediately every single time she texts, but before I can even start to think about that, I see the familiar three dots appear on my screen, and I'm laser focused on my phone. I can hear my heartbeat in my ears.

If you consider three years a minute, then yeah, definitely been a "minute."

Her dry humor makes me laugh out loud. It always has, really — Lydia has the quickest wit of anyone that

I know. She always has. I remember a specific time in college where she made me laugh so hard over a joke she made at the expense of whatever unfortunate man her sister had been dating at the time that beer came out of my nose. Something to the effect of "not being able to find something, if his track record with finding things had anything to say about it". It's good to know that even though she's been through God knows what in the past few months that she's still herself. She's still Lydia.

Beck: It's the only logical way to see it. How have you been?

Lydia: Ah, so you know about the divorce.

Lydia: What gave me away?

Lydia: Am I that transparent?

Beck: Maybe I just wanted to know how work was

Lydia: Work is work, and it's not that you're being obvious, but you forget that I know your sister.

Beck: My sister who cannot keep a secret for the life of her.

Lydia: I love her, but I also know that she called you immediately after I got off the phone with her, didn't she?

Beck: Are you shocked?

Lydia: No.

I find myself laughing yet again at this. Even though it had been years, our conversations still went like this. That we could still understand one another without really needing to try and that we could still have this kind of friendship. It, honestly, is a relief. I know that nothing could ever erase a shared childhood, an up-bringing with one another, but for as long as they were together, Tristan never really stopped trying.

It was obvious to anyone with eyes. He was intimidated by me because I knew her just as well as he did.

It was also probably obvious to anyone that I was help-lessly in love with Lydia Michaelson, and that I had been since we were kids. I tried to tell myself that I wasn't still carrying a bit of a torch for her after she got together with Tristan, but I did, all the way until I met Heather. Now, it seems as though the torch has been relit.

And the thought of that, as much as I hate to admit it, scares me a little.

Beck: So. Since we both know what I'm really asking here, then, how have you been?

Lydia: I'm managing, I guess? I rearranged my living room by myself today in an attempt to feel some-thing, so.

Lydia: Sorry, that's probably oversharing.

Beck: It's not. When Heather passed away, I got rid of all of our furniture and bought a completely new set, so I understand. Kind of.

Lydia: Beck, yours is way worse, and it's also de-pressing.

Beck: Sorry. But you're still allowed your feelings about yours.

Lydia: I know that. And I miss Heather, too, I hope you know that.

Beck: I do.

Beck: I didn't mean to compare the two.

Lydia: I know.

Beck: Sorry.

Lydia: Stop saying you're sorry, it's fine.

Beck: When people say that it just makes me want to apologize for apologizing.

Lydia: Oh, so you're one of those.

Without even realizing it, I find myself smiling again at this. It amazes me, how she does it, how she's able to take my mind off of even the worst things that I'm faced with. But it's always been this way with her. It's always been... always been this easy. And God, I missed her.

Missed this.

But I stop myself from going down this train of thought before it even has the chance to really get started. It's too soon, I remind myself, hearing my sister's voice in my ears, and I'm thankful for her sound reasoning.

Beck: You should know that about me already. I've always been a terrible people pleaser; we've known each other for years.

Lydia: Years or "minutes", as you said?

Beck: Touché. At least your sense of humor is still intact even if the rest of you is falling apart.

Lydia: Wow, I love friendship.

Lydia: Thank you for the support! (this is sarcasm, reading tone through text is hard so I felt the need to clarify)

Beck: What can I say,

Beck: I'm a stand up guy

Beck: Seriously, though, is there anything I can do to help?

Lydia: TYPING . . .

Lydia: TYPING . . .

Lydia: Do you want to help me move out of my house?

Chapter 3

Lydia

I don't know when I made the decision to sell the house. Maybe it was the first night there once the divorce was final, laying in my bed and trying to fall asleep thinking about nothing and everything all at once. Maybe it was the fifth day in a row that I had Legally Blonde on an endless loop. Maybe it was the moment I filed for divorce. But, whenever it was that the idea had come to my head, once my mind had been made up, I knew that there was no going back. I wasn't going to be able to stay here, not anymore. Not with all of the memories that stained the walls and the harrowing and deafening quiet that pervaded the entirety of every room.

Once I'd made it final, though, I didn't waste any time. I listed the house and started to sell things that I knew I wouldn't need on Facebook Marketplace (10/10 do not recommend, I underwent some very scary transactions) all in one day. And, notably, all before I figured out where I was going to be living once, I moved.

The one thing that I know for sure, though, is that I want to move back to DC. My sister and all of my closest friends are all still in the city, and I already have to commute there for work every day at the firm, so it's pretty much a no-brainer. After I make my breakfast, trying to soak up the sunny April Saturday, I start to browse apartments. But I almost choke on my morning coffee over how astronomical the price of rent for a one-bedroom apartment is, and I realize that I would likely need a roommate. Probably I should have expected this, but the fact that rent is somehow more than my mortgage payment seems especially like a crime.

"I mean, look at this," I say to my best friend, Amber, as I send her a screenshot of an apartment listing while we're on the phone, "Over $2,000 a month for a studio apartment that's barely over 400 square feet. I mean, what is this?"

"A joke. 400 square feet isn't even enough room for half of my stuff." In the background, I can hear the soothing sounds of the playlist that I know Amber plays at the yoga studio she and her wife own, aptly called The Bright Heart, between sessions. Briefly, I'm there instead of here, alone in a house that's too big for any one person to manage by themselves, surrounded by calming music and the smell of incense and doing yoga poses that I am bad at but that I know are ultimately good for me.

"Well," I start, "Maybe it'll be enough room for me, since I'm selling, like, everything I own."

"Maybe, but I am absolutely not letting you pay for that," I can tell by her tone that she is not going to relent on this matter. "It's practically a closet."

"A closet where there's no evidence that Tristan ever lived there with me," I say before I can stop myself. But I earn a laugh from Amber all the same.

"That's a good point, but still. It's highway robbery, Dee! It would make me so sad to think about you being stuck in that... that storage room. I mean, it's the principle of the thing!

You have to think about the principles."

"So, what, then?" I ask, letting out a sigh as I sink further down into the blue suede couch that I just listed on Marketplace for $200 (which I had originally bought for $1000). I realize at this moment that I also desperately need a drink. "What do you suggest I do instead?"

"I mean, you could always move in with Melanie and I." She says this like it's the simplest thing in the world, like it's as casual as asking me to go out to lunch. I pause, for a moment, trying to process exactly what she's asking me.

"What? Amber, no. I could never ask you guys to take me in like that," I insist, trying to sound firm. "You have too much on your plate."

"You're not asking, I'm offering. And besides, no one ever really stays in our guest room anyways. It's pretty much just unused space. You would be more than welcome." The gears in my head turn as I try to make sense of this incredibly selfless and deeply kind offer. I don't know the last time someone has done something like this for me, and it almost knocks me off balance.

I'm quiet for a moment as I think.

"Well, I would need to pay you for it," I insist, "You can't let me live there for free."

"I would, though, it really doesn't make a difference either way."

"It makes a difference to me. Let me pay you."

"You seriously don't have to—"

"How much is your rent per month?" I cut her off when I ask, but I don't apologize, even when I hear her sigh through the speaker. I know that it's the least I can do, to pay my share and to contribute to the place where I will be living. I wouldn't feel right about staying with her otherwise.

"$3,570, but seriously, there's two of us already—"

"So, I pay you, like, $1,785 and you're also saving me almost $500 per month. If you're serious about this, I have to pay you guys. I can't just take it as a handout. It would make me feel so terrible, because I don't need a free place to live, I just need someplace to live. And I will move out as soon as I find a place that's actually decent. Once I'm... once I'm back on my feet." Amber is quiet for a moment as she considers this, and I hear the low hum of the instrumental music in the background.

"If we're splitting rent, there's no way I'm letting you pay more than a third when there are two of us and only one of you. $1,190 and not a cent more, okay?"

"Amber, I—"

"Lydia, please. I want you to come live with me. It's not charity, it's friendship, and that's why I invited you. Please let me do this thing for you. Please." Another beat passes. Her kindness has stunned me into silence. Suddenly, I find myself very interested in a string hanging off of the couch that I hadn't noticed before. I pick at it, and I wonder if Tristan had ever noticed it, and then I'm all the more eager to sell this house and every piece of furniture in it. So, I sigh and nod, even though she can't see me, and I finally speak. "Okay."

"Good!" Amber chirps, and I can tell that her excitement isn't feigned or disingenuous. It's almost too easy to picture her standing up, hands clasped and a beaming smile on her face as she's saying it. Her mannerisms are like second nature to me at this point in our friendship, so I wouldn't be surprised if that was exactly what she was doing. "I'm so excited, you have no idea! I know Melanie will be too; she misses you. It'll be like old times, all of us back in the same city again." This last part brings a bittersweet smile to my face. I catch a glimpse of a framed photo on the mantle of the four of us from our last trip as high school seniors before college; Me, Olivia, Beck, and Amber stand sunburnt and giddy on a dock down at their family's old beach house in Florida, at

Cape San Blas. None of us had a care in the world other than being around the people who we loved most.

I remember as we stood there, smiling for the picture and squinting against the bright sunlight reflecting off the clear blue water, thinking that I likely wouldn't ever be as happy as I was then again. I also remember the mischievous smile on Beck's face as I looked up at him, his skin sun kissed with freckles dotting his nose and his hair wild and a brighter blonde than usual from the saltwater. It was like I knew what he was going to do before he did it, because we had that kind of a connection. And as soon as the camera shutter flickered, he picked me up and threw me in the water like it was nothing. My clothes were soaked, and I feigned anger at him, but jumped out and tackled him in with me. We stayed out there until sunset, laughing and swimming between drinks and breaks for snacks and beach games.

Life was so much simpler back then.

"Like old times," I finally say, and I can only hope that in at least some capacity, that I can somehow find my way back to that happy girl that I used to be.

***

A week later, I find myself in a U-Haul driving all of the furniture that I hadn't sold with me into the city and towards Amber and Melanie's apartment. I've pretty much resigned myself to moving all of the big pieces that haven't sold yet into storage, but that'll be a problem for another day. The moving crew I hired had been efficient enough in packing the stuff up, and the house would be professionally cleaned by the time that my real estate agent would start showing it. So, I assure myself, there really isn't much more that I can do for myself at this moment. I am out of that place and won't ever have to live in that house again.

There wasn't ever really an option to wait on the house to sell before I moved. Not in my mind, at least. Just as much as there wasn't an option not to talk to Beck about it all. Letting myself think back on the time we used to spend together made me realize just how stupid I had been to let someone else tell me who I could or couldn't be friends with, and that it was far past time for Beck and I to reconnect.

And what I'd realized after I texted him was that I missed him. Far more than I ever could have expected.

The drive from my house right outside of Potomac to DC proper isn't much more than 20 minutes, give or take a bit of time with traffic. The rolling green hills are broken up by houses and trees and the occasional house. The closer to the city I get, though, the buildings become more dense, the architecture older and more stately. To my dismay, though, the traffic also gets so much worse due to the endless stream of tourists. Even still, I've missed it here — I missed our days at GW and the hidden study spots that I would find deep in the halls of the MLK Library that we would stay in for God knows how long.

I missed this place. I can't believe that I ever left.

It's well past lunchtime by the time that I finally arrive. I send a quick text to Amber, letting her know that I've made it safely, and pull around to her building once she lets me in the gate. Her apartment complex seems to have gotten a bit of a facelift since the last time I was here — the previously red portions of brick exterior have all been painted white, which I silently chuckle at. Seems to be everyone's idea of a renovation nowadays. Whatever else they did on the outside, though, really elevated the place, and I'm almost too busy admiring all the updates to notice when Amber comes running down the steps to greet me. I park the truck and smile at her through the window, giving a small wave before I jump down out of the driver's seat and wrap her in a hug. Her long red hair threatens to swat me in the face as she grabs me for a hug, and she smells exactly like I remember, vanilla and patchouli.

"Oh my God! Look at you!" She practically squeals, pulling away just enough to rest her hands on my shoulders. The cheerful sparkle in her eye is completely the opposite from her somewhat impish smile. "Divorce suits you, you look so hot, you've got that beautiful, divorced lady glow." When I laugh at this, I actually snort, and simultaneously wonder how long it's been since I let myself genuinely laugh like that.

"I'm sorry, what? I'm divorced, not pregnant, that doesn't come with a glow."

"It does when it comes to you, obviously!"

"You'll have to forgive her," Melanie says, having finally walked up behind Amber. I'm always struck by how different the two of them are, how they're basically the poster child for a couple with black cat and golden retriever energy. Melanie's cool confidence gives the impression that she was never really self-conscious about her style and always wanted to express herself through it, meaning dark hair and plenty of jewelry. I love Melanie. "She thinks she's funny, but she's really just crass and a little rude."

"Hey." Amber pouts playfully as she leans into Melanie's side where her arm has slid around her waist.

"I'm just teasing." I find my smile growing wider by the minute while I'm around them.

"Trust me," I assure her, raising my eyebrows for emphasis, "I know all about Amber's terrible humor. I was cursed with it long before you came along." This earns me a laugh from Melanie, but Amber playfully gives me the finger, and I laugh even harder at that. Then, I hear a car door close behind me.

"Who's got terrible humor? Amber?" I hear my sister's voice before I see her face. I hadn't even noticed that they had been parking. I knew she would be here around the same time as me but seeing her again after nearly two months grounds me, and I have to stop my eyes from welling up with tears as I start towards her. Another car door closes, and my sister's new fiancée, Thomas, climbs out of the passenger seat.

"It's definitely Amber," He agrees teasingly, but I don't pay him much attention at first. Instead, I run to my sister, throwing my arms around her and hugging her wordlessly. She hugs back, like she knows it's exactly what I need at this moment.

"Okay, who else has something to say about my jokes? Anyone?" Amber says, finally breaking the silence as I finally break from my hug with Olivia, our arms still firmly around one another. Thomas and I nod at each other in greeting, and he ruffles my hair, which only endears me towards him even further. The handful of times I have met him, we've really gotten to bond, and I'm so glad that my sister found her perfect match in him. "If you do, get it all out now, before I kick literally all of you out of my home. Melanie included."

"Ouch," Melanie replies through a laugh, "What did I do?"

"I was only teasing too." I turn my attention back to Amber when I say this, while still remaining firmly planted at my sister's side. We laugh together, and I open my free arm for her, the three of us standing there for a moment and hugging one another the same way we had since we were children. All of us, together. It has always just been better that way. "You know I love you. God, is it just me, or have they worked on this place since the last time I was here?"

"No, they gave it all a total facelift," Amber nods, confirming my suspicions. "Rent prices started to skyrocket and they wanted to get in on the inflation action."

"Yay, capitalism." My voice is completely devoid of humor. That inflation is what got me into this mess, anyway — of having to choose between having roommates when I'm nearly thirty or paying more than a mortgage payment for a place that's practically a shoebox. "Anyway, we should probably get to it. Anyone wanna help me back this truck up?"

"I can help with that," I hear a voice say from behind me, then. A voice I would recognize anywhere. I'd been swinging the U-Haul keys around and around my finger in a bit of a fidget, but I let them fall still as I turn around, my restlessness being outweighed by my need to see him.

A lot can change in three years. I'm acutely aware of this, but what strikes me most about Beck is how much has stayed the same. When he walks towards me and opens his arms, he still wears that same goofy smile he's always had. His cheeks still dimple in exactly the same places.

He's as tall as he was before, which isn't shocking, but he's definitely broader, larger in every sense of the word. The boy who I had once known to be awkward and lanky with his height had grown into a man, and a very good man at that. He had a bit of light stubble accenting his cheekbones too that tickles the side of my face when he scoops down to wrap me in one of his bear hugs.

"Hey, Dee." He's so warm, and he smells exactly the same, and I am racking my brain for why on Earth it is that I didn't notice how handsome he is before. I think that on some level I already knew that I was subconsciously aware of it. Or maybe that I knew it as a matter of fact rather than as an opinion, like how you're aware that someone is attractive conventionally, but it doesn't necessarily mean that you're attracted to them. But one thing is for certain, and it is that when I am hugging Beck Shepherd, his attractiveness is fully, consciously an opinion.

And God, am I in trouble.

Chapter 4

Beck

I didn't know how much seeing Lydia in person would actually affect me until it happened. I'd seen some photos online of all the vacations that she had gone on or events she'd gone to; The first thing that I notice, though, is that she cut her hair shorter than it's ever been. Her hair is just barely below her collarbone. She'd always kept her hair long in the past, her honey-brown waves falling all the way down her back, and it makes her look more mature, older than the little girl I remember growing up with.

God, she's stunning.

After we greet each other, I'm quiet for the rest of the time we're unloading the U-Haul. I've always been a lot more introverted than most of my friends, Lydia included, but I'm especially stuck in my own head as the conversation ebbs and flows. I try to keep up, try to chime in as I'm hoisting boxes and boxes of Lydia's clothes into Amber and Melanie's guest room. A comment here and there about Thomas' tuxedo preferences for the wedding or about how Melanie rearranged the living room again (I almost tripped over an ottoman that hadn't been there the last time I visited), but for the most part, I let everyone else lead the conversation.

All I can focus on is Lydia.

Eventually, everything is unloaded that's not going to have to go to the storage unit Lydia rented, and is shoved into what's now going to be her bedroom. She insists she can unpack it and arrange things herself, and Thomas brings up the idea of going out for dinner and drinks. Everyone agrees before I can even think about what I'm signing myself up for, but even though my social battery is teetering on empty, I agree to go, if only because it means I'll get to spend more time with Lydia.

"So who's driving?" Amber asks as we stand together outside her apartment. I think that I could probably melt from how sweaty I am. The southern humidity has not been kind to us this afternoon, so I'm looking forward to having a beer in a place where there's air conditioning. "Do we need to take multiple cars?"

"I can drive—" "I'll just ride with Beck—" Lydia and I chime in, speaking over one another. I can't fight back the smile that threatens to creep its way across my face, a bit of introversion kicking in as I avert my gaze downward. I'm sure that I'm blushing, but if I know anything about Lydia, she is too. At least we're on the same page about having some time to catch up with each other after so long. I catch Melanie's eye then, a knowing grin on her features.

"Well okay then." Melanie raises her eyebrows at me when she says this. I love my sister in law, but she's just as bad as Amber is sometimes when it comes to teasing me.

"Well, that was easy," Olivia says, breaking the tension, "Thomas and I can just ride with you guys."

Thomas places a gentle hand on Olivia's back. "Did you invite Callie? I invited Mason."

"Done and done," Olivia nods. They exchange a look, and if what I've gathered from Amber is correct, they're running a little scheme to get the two of them together. I've never met either of them, but know that Mason was Thomas' roommate before Thomas and Olivia got engaged.

" That's still going on?" Amber asks pointedly, "Wow, you're persistent."

"Listen, they're meant to be," Olivia waves her off, confirming my suspicions. "They just don't know it yet." Beside me, Lydia rolls her eyes playfully, folding her arms across her chest as she does so.

"Trust her, she's the creator of Small & Sparkling ," Lydia says with a flourish of her hands, her tone dripping with sarcasm, "She just knows these things." If Olivia is bothered by her younger sister's teasing, she doesn't show it, laughing and playfully punching her arm.

"Yeah, and now that I have my own success story to show for it, I'm pretty much everyone's favorite romance guru." Lydia scoffs at this, and Olivia shoots me a wink, letting me know that her sarcasm is as thinly veiled as I suspected. "Anyways, where do we want to go?"

"What about Callaghan's?" Thomas suggests.

"Ooh, I love Callaghan's," Melanie says, and for a moment, I consider the possibility that it's the most cheerful I've ever seen her. "I could go for a Guinness." Amber wrinkles her nose a little at this, and I laugh. My sister and her wife represent the very definition of the idea that opposites attract.

"Oh, come on," Melanie continues, "Going to an Irish pub and not ordering a pint should be a crime. What are you gonna get, then? Something pink and disgusting?"

"Rosé, thank you very much. It's summer, the heat is killing me, and beer is gross." Amber says definitively, tilting her chin up in a defiant way that I recognize from our shared childhood.

Olivia nods her approval. "Speak your truth."

"Are we all just going to stand here talking about how fucking hot it is now that we've been moving all day," Lydia says then, and I'm silently thankful that she decided to break up this conversation, because it really is becoming unbearably hot, "Or do you guys actually want to go get a drink and stop making me suffer?"

"Alright, alright," Olivia concedes, "We'll see you guys there, okay?"

Once we're on the way to the pub, the first half of the drive is mostly silent. I keep my eyes trained on the road, for the most part, thankful for the fact that my car has decent AC. But every now and again, I spare a glance in Lydia's direction. She's looking out the window, watching the trees and the buildings pass by as we near downtown. Once we get closer to the most populated part of the city, traffic (of course) starts to get more dense. We reach 14th street, with all of its apartment buildings towering tall and restaurants lining the sidewalks, and we slow to a speed that's nearly just a stop. Vienna by Billy Joel hums through the speakers of my Bronco, and I'm drumming my thumbs on the steering wheel, when I finally work up the nerve to talk.

"So, how have you been—" "Amber and Melanie's place—" Laughter breaks the air of tension between us as we find ourselves speaking over each other for the second time that day. I'm thankful that it's not awkward. It's more funny than anything else, the fact that we're still so in sync even after so many years separated.

"Sorry, you go first," I say then, smiling over at her for a moment.

"No, you can," Lydia counters, matching my smile.

"I insist."

"Amber and Melanie's place is a lot bigger than I remember."

"Oh, yeah," I agree, craning my neck a little bit to try and see if there's a break in traffic anywhere before the parking deck we're headed towards (there's not). "Melanie had Amber get rid of a bunch of the trinkets and statues and lamps and things that were taking up space in there." I leave out the part where I had to be over there in the dead heat of last Summer helping them move it all.

"It's nice. It's still got character, but I don't feel like I'm going to trip when I walk in."

"I still tripped anyways." I laugh at myself when I say it. "But I see your point."

"I wasn't even going to bring that up. But now that you did, you basically looked like a cartoon character trying not to fall. Windmill arms and all." My laughter grows louder, and the sound of Lydia's laughter follows. A beat of silence passes between us, then, and in it hangs the heavy weight of so many words unsaid, of years of friendship followed by years of near nothingness , of a wanting that, for all I knew, went unreciprocated for the entirety of our childhood.

But this is Lydia, I remind myself. Lydia, who you used to make fairy potions with out of moss and pond water. Lydia, who you threw off your parent's dock into the clear blue water of St. Joseph Bay . So I press on, my missing her outweighing the confusing tide of emotions that threatens to make me retreat even further into myself.

"So," I say, clearing my throat, "How have you been?"

"Oh, you know. It could be worse. I could have had to undergo an ice pick lobotomy in the 1930's or something." I laugh again, grateful for Lydia's ability to keep things light. "I'm doing about... as well as can be expected, though. Tristan has finally started to leave me alone a bit more now that the divorce is final, which has been a relief."

"What was he doing before?"

"Oh, you know. Drunk calls, texts begging for my forgiveness that were also probably fueled by drunkenness. Same shit you'd expect from an alcoholic." She gives me a self-pitying laugh and a bit of a shrug, grimacing a bit at herself. I can tell that she feels about as awkward as I do at this long-awaited reunion, and I feel the need to prove to her that I'm still me, that this can still be as easy as it was before the years of not speaking. "Sorry. Probably I'm oversharing."

"You're not. I'm sorry."

"It's fine. I'm really happy for Liv, though," She says, shooting me a wide smile, "I'm going to be her Maid of Honor."

"I honestly wouldn't have expected anything else."

"Well, I would have been Matron instead of Maid, if I were still married — sorry. I need to stop trying to cope with humor." Lydia groans when she says this, burying her face in her hands.

"No, it's fine, I make dead wife jokes sometimes," I blurt out before I can stop myself, cringing and pursing my lips together. "God, I'm a horrible person. I only make them in my head, I promise." Lydia is quiet for a moment, looking over at me with an expression that's a mix of pitying and understanding.

"Wow, you suck," She says after a moment, a laugh following her teasing words. I laugh again, grateful for

Lydia's expert skill at diffusing tension. "I feel way better about my terrible coping skills now."

"Glad I could be of service," I say, and a smile is exchanged between the two of us. Vienna fades out, and I hear the opening notes of Rocketman start. This had always been a favorite of mine, ever since we were kids, and I know that Lydia remembers this, because she raises her eyebrows when she hears it. "Seriously, though, are you okay?"

"I'm... I'm trying my best."

"That's all you can do."

"I'm thinking about taking a leave of absence from work, though." This admission stops me in my tracks. I furrow my eyebrows as I look over at her.

"What? Didn't you just make junior partner?" If there's one thing that I have always known about Lydia, it's that she's dedicated to her work. She's always been one of the most career-driven ones out of all of us, and I admired her greatly for it, so hearing that she needed a break from it was all of the confirmation that I needed to know that she really was having a harder time than she let on.

"Yeah, but that promotion gives me a lot more freedom to kind of... do what I want. I can work remotely, too, but what I really want to do is travel. Places that I want to go to." She says this last bit with conviction, like it's the most important thing to her. "It's been too long since I've made the decisions about my own trip."

"I think that's great," I say honestly, and she smiles at me gently. "You should do it."

"Yeah, I'm working on it."

Once we finally park, we walk the half mile distance to the pub, exchanging jokes and memories of our childhoods spent together. The setting sun and the shade from the trees lining the street have offered us a brief reprieve from the heat. Coupled with a slow breeze, the evening seems to be shaping up to be far kinder to us than the sweltering warmth of the day.

Callaghan's is tucked unsuspectingly between a barber shop and a boutique on the corner of 14th street. On the outside, it looks far smaller than either of the other two establishments, and you're likely to walk right past it if you're not paying attention. A small entry hallway to the bar and the row of booths are what you're greeted with when you walk in. Neon signs and license plates from various states plaster the walls, as well as various renditions of the Irish flag and a couple of framed photos of Barack Obama. I asked one of the bartenders about it once, and apparently there's some gas station in Ireland that's completely themed after the Obama family, complete with a statue of him in front. I had to look it up before I believed him, but it turns out that it's real, and so I stopped questioning it.

The real secret to Callaghan's, though, is the back deck. Once you walk past the small indoor seating area, consisting only of the bar and the only stretch of tables directly across from it, you get to the back of the restaurant, where a pair of glass doors ushers you into the fully air-conditioned open back patio. It's about three times the size of the inside, with another outdoor bar and plenty of high-top tables. String lights cascade across the beams of wood that provide structure to the shade canopies, and at the very back is a small stage where live musicians play every Friday and Saturday. Somehow, the entirety of the deck is also surrounded by trees, keeping it perfectly cool even in the hottest summer months.

I wave a greeting to the bartender who's at the outdoor bar as we walk out onto the patio. Ryan, I recall, and I remember that he'd been the one to tell me about the Barack Obama gas station. I kind of hope that he comes and talks to us, and that he can tell Lydia about it, because I noticed a puzzled look on her face when we walked past the photos. I also quickly spot our group, seated at our favorite circular table in the corner. I wave to them in greeting, placing a gentle hand on Lydia's shoulder as we walk in their direction and trying to ignore the surge of electricity that courses through me just from touching her.

"Wow, this place is great," Lydia says, "When did you guys find it?"

"A couple of years ago. Olivia really hasn't taken you here when you've visited the city?"

"Oh. Well, I guess not... Tristan typically liked to make the decisions when it came to restaurants."

"Ah, so he was a loser who didn't like bar food, got it." At this, she laughs and gives me a playful nudge with her elbow. I pull out her chair for her when we sit, the waiter coming to take our drink orders pretty quickly after we exchange greetings with everyone. Olivia, Thomas Amber, & Melanie have beat us to the restaurant, but we're not the last to arrive — I take note that there are still two empty seats at the end of the table, which I can only assume will belong to Callie and Mason. Convenient that they decided to leave those two seats open like that, I think, so they'd be forced to sit next to each other. They really are a bunch of schemers.

Before Lydia and I's drinks are brought out, Callie arrives, followed shortly by Mason. I can tell that she's just as suspicious as I was about the seating arrangement as soon as she sits down, planting herself next to Lydia and hugging her in greeting so that the seat next to Thomas is left open for Mason. Smart , I think, gives her plenty of reason to ignore him if he wants. When Mason walks in, he's every bit as handsome and frat president material as I imagined for someone with a name like his, brown hair that's perfectly styled and blue eyes and dimples. He gives Thomas a firm handshake in greeting and ruffles Callie's hair petulantly, before finally pausing to look in my direction.

"Woah, who's the new guy?" He asks, grinning over at me as he sits.

"Mase, I love you, but you are without a doubt the new guy here," Olivia starts with a chiding grin. "Me and Lydia go way back with Beck and Amber."

"Well, I don't play for the same team, but if I did, damn, " Mason jokes, and I have to stifle a laugh as Callie rolls her eyes and punches him in the shoulder playfully. "What? I'm serious. I mean, look at the man, he's practically a Greek god."

"You do realize that I'm right here, right?"

"I would say it to your face, and I am saying it to your face. You, my friend, are a gorgeous hunk of man. How are you not off the market yet?"

"Mason, easy," Lydia chimes in, "Down boy." I can tell that she's joking, but she's also simultaneously diverting the topic from my relationship status so that I don't have to tell this

relative stranger the history of how I became a widower before the time I turned 30. For that, I'm grateful, and I shoot her a knowing glance of appreciation as the waiter collects Mason and Callie's drink orders.

"Fine, fine, the name's Mason, but I guess you already knew that, since Lydia just said it."

"Nice to finally meet you," I say, reaching behind the girls to shake his hand.

"Likewise. And the violent little five foot blonde that just punched me is Callie." Callie cocks her head at him, then, every bit the picture of the precocious spitfire that she's been made out to be by my sister and her friends.

"I am perfectly capable of introducing myself," She insists as she folds her arms across her chest.

"I know, but I didn't know if your idea of a proper greeting was a swift kick to the shin, considering how combative you've been so far tonight. Figured I would save the man some pain."

"Fuck off," Callie bites back, and they stick their tongues out at each other like a couple of arguing pre-schoolers. I see it, then, what everyone else sees — he's a little boy pulling a girl's pigtails on the playground to get her attention because he thinks she's pretty. Clearly, they're made for each other. And, as a bonus, they're both gorgeous, so it works.

"Mom, Dad, stop fighting!" Olivia jokes, sipping her wine.

"I don't know if 'Dad' works for Mason," Thomas muses, acting as though he's thinking very hard about this comparison. "He's more like that weird uncle that you only see at Thanksgiving and Christmas. 'Oh, there's Drunk Uncle Randy, who do you guys think he's going to throw up on this time?"

Mason scoffs dramatically as the waiter returns to place his and Callie's drinks down in front of them. "What is this, the roast of Mason? I didn't sign up for this."

Amber shakes her head, looking over at Lydia point-edly. "No, this is still Operation Celebrate Lydia's Freedom and Return To Us By Getting Blind Drunk on a Tuesday."

"Wow, long title," I whistle, "We can't call it something else? At least for the toast? I don't know if I can remember all of that."

"Fine. To Lydia!" Amber calls, and we all raise our glasses. A chorus of "Lydia!" rings out across the table, and we clink our glasses together with the people closest to us.

Mason joins in slightly late, though, his beer bottle raised high triumphantly over his head with a cheer of "She's single and ready to mingle!"

"Okay, I don't know about 'mingle'," Lydia laughs.

"She's single and ready to daydream about various men!" We all laugh and cheer again at this, sipping our drinks in celebration.

The evening starts to pass in a haze of drinks and raucous laughter. I probably shouldn't be surprised at how well Mason, Callie, and Thomas fit in with the rest of our little group, but they're as natural an addition as Melanie was once, she and Amber found one another. But I can't help but feel a little pang of nostalgia-fueled sadness at how bittersweet it all is; It used to only be the four of us, and now we've all grown and changed and gotten older, and it's a little difficult to reconcile, for some reason. Maybe it's the distance I had from Lydia for a while, maybe it's the alcohol, but the inevitability of change threatens the happiness that I feel, making this reunion with her feel fragile and somewhat fleeting, even though I know it's not.

But I see it in the people around me, the ones she's known for at least a couple of years now. Her life moved on without me in it. How does someone come to terms with that kind of thing?

I try to keep myself from retreating inside my own mind for the rest of the night, chiming into conversations when I can. We eat, we talk, and we laugh, and then I find myself looking over at Amber. There's a mischievous look on her face, and she grins at me — in that moment, I realize that she's up to something, what she brought Lydia here for.

"So. Lydia," She starts, "I did have an ulterior motive in bringing you here."

"Oh no," Lydia groans, but the smile on her face reveals her playful nature. "Should I be scared? Are you going to ask me to help you hide my ex-husband's body or something?"

"No, but that would have been a good idea too. Okay, here we go. Drumroll! Melanie, do a drumroll." Melanie obliges, drumming her hands against the table. Her eyes plead for help from the rest of us, and so we all join in; I pat my hands on the tops of my thighs, Callie uses a couple of straws, and Mason chimes in with a "Duh-duh-duh-duh-duh" that is louder than the rest of what we're doing. Then, Amber produces two slips of paper from her purse — plane tickets, and slides them across the table to Lydia.

"Ta-da!" She cheers, clasping her hands together in front of her gleefully. I turn to gauge Lydia's reaction to our surprise, but at first, her expression is unreadable. Her brow furrows, her gaze flickering from the tickets to all of us and back to the tickets.

"Amber, what is this?" She says finally, voice full of confusion and emotion.

Then, I see it — the slightest indication of unease in her eyes, and I lace my hands together so hard to keep myself from grabbing hers that my knuckles turn white.

Chapter 5

Lydia

"What?" At first, I don't think I'm hearing her correctly. A one-week reprieve from my life, all paid for, at one of my favorite places in the world, followed up by a dream vacation of mine to Greece for six days and five nights. The memories that I have at Amber and Beck's beach house are some of those core memories that you never let go of, the ones that hold onto you in your darkest times and carry you through them. Memories of friendships being built, of moments that sparked my love of travel, of evenings spent around kitchen tables playing card games and the only somewhat inevitable family scuffle when someone was a sore loser.

Going back to the cape seems halfway like it would be the answer to all of my problems, and halfway like it would do nothing but send me even further into a spiral, making me long for the freedom of childhood and the simplicity of a life before Tristan.

"I said it's all taken care of, Lydia," Amber says again, and I notice her expression waver slightly, her gleeful anticipation being replaced by quiet concern. "We all... We all pitched in.

You need this. Let us do this for you."

I think back, then, about all of the times that I had dreamed about going to Greece. About how much I must have talked about it to Amber, to Olivia, about this very trip and the merits of it. About how it's a perfect mix of adventurous and historic, of relaxing and fun. I have always loved to travel, which was the one thing that Tristan and I really connected on when we first started dating. But once we were married, he always claimed to know best about our destinations, about making the plans for where we should go.

Still, no matter how eager I might actually be to do something like this, I shudder to think about what they must have collectively spent on it, on me. I don't necessarily have concerns about money following the divorce, and the only logical solution right now seems to be to give them back every single cent they'd put forward towards it all.

"Amber, this — it's too much," I say, shaking my head and swallowing. I feel the hot sting of tears that threaten to creep into my eyes from the overwhelm. "I can't just... accept this from you without giving you anything back. It feels like charity."

"It's not. It's a gift," She says, and I take pause for a second before I realize what she means. "An early birthday gift."

I had been so focused on the divorce proceedings and all of the surrounding drama and the chaos of moving that I had created for myself that I completely neglected to remember that my birthday was in two weeks. My 29th birthday. The last year of my twenties had crept up on me without warning and is now being colored by a divorce and the subsequent upheaval of my entire life.

Even so, it would be a lie for me to say that I didn't want to go on the trip, because I did, I really did. And I know that they all knew, since I had talked about Greece with most of them at length. But I figured that the least I could do was pay them back, at least in some amount.

"Well, it's too much," I persist, "I just — you have to let me give you something. You have to let me pay for something ."

Melanie laughs at this. "If you want to figure out how to pay all of us whatever sum you deem appropriate, good luck, because that's going to be a lot of math."

"Dude, I hate math," Mason groans, polishing off his beer, "Just save yourself the trouble and go have fun." I blink in surprise at this — I hadn't expected Mason to chime into this conversation. He's a nice person, but we don't know each other as well as he knows the others.

"Wait," I say, turning my attention to him, "Did you contribute to this too?"

"Oh. Uh, a little," Mason confirms, cheeks a slight tinge of pink as he looks down at his now empty glass. I can tell he's a bit embarrassed by my line of questioning, so I back off. "But not as much as like, your sister and all those other guys. I mean, we've only met each other a couple times." I'm quiet for another moment. Here is this person who I am only friends with by happenstance, who the people who love me had recruited to help them out for this, for me . And he had wanted to.

"Shit," I mutter. It feels all-encompassing and completely correct towards how I feel about the situation. But, since I can't put all of that into words without rambling all night (and because my head is light and swimmy from the alcohol), all I say next is, "That would be a lot of math."

"My point exactly," Melanie nods at me in solidarity.

"So... what, then?" I ask, trying to make sense of all of this through my wine-stained consciousness. "You said the trip was for two, right? Are you coming with me, Amber?"

"Well... I was going to," Amber starts, a gentle smile playing on her lips as she reaches across the table for Melanie's hand. "But I can't exactly afford to take time off of work anymore right now."

"Why? What's going on? Is everything... is everything okay?" The last thing that I want is to know that they're financially burdened by the fact that I've moved in with them somehow, that this trip was harder on them than they thought it was going to be.

"Oh! Yeah, it's nothing like that, I promise. It's... We're..."

"We're starting the adoption process," Melanie says, and Amber's smile splits her face wide.

"Holy shit!" Olivia shouts, grabbing Thomas' forearm for support as she leans forward excitedly.

"Oh my God, Amber!" I stand up, moving over to her to hug them both. My sister joins me, and we stay there for a moment, hugging and laughing as the others take their turns congratulating Melanie and Amber. "So, I mean, Liv? Do you think you could come with me?"

"Well, I was going to try," She starts, a look of regret already present on her face, "But with all of the S&S stuff recently and the wedding planning, I just can't take the time off."

"Oh." A beat of silence passes. And then it hits me all at once — everyone is moving on.

Everyone is living their lives, having kids, and getting married. But what about me?

Well, I'm junior partner at the firm.

But I've taken so many steps backwards in just a year. I'm single again, I'm starting over completely, kids are nowhere in sight for me anymore. Once, that had been me, starting out with so much promise. But now, here I am, back at square one. Starting over when I'm nearly 30.

"I just... I guess I could go alone?" I say after a moment, but the hesitancy must be obvious in my voice, because I catch Beck looking over at me, concern etched across his features. "I don't know, I've never really felt safe traveling alone though —"

"I'll go with you," Beck chimes in, definitive and resolute.

"What?" His decisiveness disarms me for a moment. "You... Beck, really? You will?"

"Yeah. I mean, I paid for part of the vacation anyways," He says, offering me a shrug and a smile, like it's the most simple decision he's ever made. "It's really not a big deal."

"What about... you have work too, don't you?" I feel a tentative smile forming on my face — this might actually happen. This might be real.

"I have time off that I haven't taken yet this year. And I intend to use it. Really, I don't mind missing work. At all."

"There you go!" Amber claps, wrapping me up in another hug. "Gosh, wait, that's so perfect. It's really going to be just like old times now! You guys are going to have so much fun."

Like old times . I would give anything to go back there, back to when things were easier and I wasn't ending up sad and alone.

Maybe, if I pretend enough, it really will be like old times.

Amber keeps us all out for more drinks for roughly another hour after we finish eating. By the time we're all saying our goodbyes at the cars and going our separate ways, I've had at least two more drinks, and my mind is absolutely racing. I'm struck with so many negative thoughts about all I am going to have to start over with while simultaneously being hit with waves of childhood nostalgia, of melting popsicles on Beck's dock and games of Marco Polo in the bay. When I go to find Beck after saying goodbye to Amber, he must notice that something is off, because he grabs me by the shoulders, looking me in the eyes.

"Hey. What's wrong?"

"Nothing," I lie, even though I'm pretty sure his hands are the only thing keeping me upright, "I'm fine."

"Well, that's a lie."

Damn. He sees right through me, and I hate it.

"I wish you could at least pretend you don't know me as well for once. It's been three years, Beck, there's plenty you don't know." My words are sharp, biting. They're entirely too harsh, but I can't stop them before they're out. I look at Beck, then, his expression unreadable when my eyes meet his.

"Lydia, trust me. I know how long it's been," He starts, and I notice the quiver in his voice when he speaks, the shake in his breath when he inhales. "I've spent three years missing you. You don't have to remind me of any of that, I'm perfectly aware."

His words hit me like a blow to the chest, threatening to knock me over. Definitely I'm already unsteady from the alcohol, but my head swims from the force of the admission. Beck had missed me for three years, for the entire time we'd been apart, and I had a sneaking suspicion it wasn't in a way that was strictly friendly. Maybe it's because of the way he's looking at me, or maybe it's in the tension that I notice in the air.

Or maybe it's something that's been building for years, simmering just under the surface, threatening to boil over and consume both of us.

Either way, silence stretches between the two of us as we stand in front of Beck's car, and it is almost deafening. Electricity courses through me when I catch the way he's looking at me, taking me in; If it were anyone but Beck, I would think they were checking me out.

Oh my God, is Beck checking me out? Or is my drunk mind playing tricks on me?

"Beck," I say then, before I even realize what's going to come out of my mouth next, "Beck, take me home." He sighs, nodding and pushing a hand through his sandy curls.

"Okay," he says, moving around me to open the car door for me, clearly missing the meaning that I was trying to convey with my words. When he puts his hand on the small of my back to reach around me, I turn and face him, emboldened by our proximity as I press my hand against his chest, taking in a sharp breath as I look up at him.

"No, Beck. I mean... take me home. With you."

He pauses, for a moment. I notice his eyes flicking from mine to my lips and then back to my eyes. Beck's throat works as he swallows, and he looks for a moment like a man starved, like he needed something badly and had for quite some time. Before I fully process what's going on, before I have even half a second to regret it, he leans in.

Beck Shepherd presses his lips against mine, hard and deliberate, and I know that he's just getting started.

Chapter 6

Beck

The drive back to my place from Callaghan's is almost torturously long, but not long enough for me to reconsider what's about to happen. Not when I've finally had a taste of the girl of my dreams and she's looking at me like she never has before. I'm already a bit of a mess, my hair disheveled from where her hands had been and my breath still somewhat ragged as we drive, mostly in silence, the low hum of my radio playing Wild Horses by The Rolling Stones the only thing breaking through the silence.

Then, as soon as we're out of the car and inside, I spin around, closing the door and pinning Lydia against it, my lips finding hers. It's not hurried, but it's purposeful, and I know for a fact that now that I've gotten started I won't be able to stop. She parts her lips for me, and I groan, fully conscious of the fact that this woman could bring me to my knees in no more than a second should

I fully give in. Her hands find their way into my hair again, tugging and pulling at the waves, and I know that my desire for her must be obvious as I press my torso and my hips flush against hers. If she minds, though, she doesn't show it, because she lets out a little whimper when I slip my tongue into her mouth, moving her body languidly to grind her hips against mine.

"Fuck," I manage, letting out a throaty groan that Lydia eagerly swallows. "Lydia, please." Her hands move from my hair so that she can throw her arms around my neck, a leg hooking around my waist like she wants to climb me.

"More," She breathes against my lips, pushing her chest firmly against mine as she rolls her hips again. The feeling of her breasts pressing against me like this is enough to make me lightheaded. "I need more of you, Beck."

"Easy," I say then with a low chuckle, as a gentle prompting, steadying myself so that she doesn't knock me down. My lips brush against hers as I speak, and it sends a chill through every inch of me. "You're gonna take us both to the floor if you're not careful."

"Who says I don't want that?"

I let out another strangled noise of want at her urgency. As much as her eagerness makes me want to give her exactly what she wants, taking her then and there against the hardwoods, I've waited too long for this moment. I'm going to do this right, so the first time that I'm sleeping with Lydia will not be happening on my living room floor. Maybe we can get there later, though, I reason with myself. I lift her up effortlessly then, scooping her into my arms. A small sound of surprise passes her lips as I carry her bridal-style into my bedroom, before kicking the door closed behind us and placing her down on the bed gently.

I watch her as she props herself up on her elbows, eyes full of mischief with a wicked grin plastered across her face; My eyes stay locked on hers as I pull my shirt over my head eagerly with one hand, tossing it to the floor. Lydia's chest heaves a bit as she takes in a sharp breath — I don't know what it is at first, but as I realize she's taking me in, looking me up and down with this look of pure desire in her eyes, I groan, palming myself through my jeans in search of friction.

"Take your shirt off," I tell her directly, "Now." Then, I watch as she unwraps herself like a present for me. In the dim lamplight, she looks like something out of a painting, like she's too angelic to be human. I crawl over the top of her, then, reaching around her back to unclasp her bra as I kiss her hungrily. Lydia responds in kind, hands roaming up and down my now bare chest. I find myself completely pliant, putty in her hands as she traces her fingertips down my torso delicately. My hips roll against hers again, involuntarily this time, and she lets out the smallest whimper and another plea for more. I reach up, cupping one of her breasts in my hand and moaning into her mouth. I pinch her nipple, then, only slightly, and she keens for me, so I know I'm on the right track.

"You're so beautiful," I say then, voice nearly hoarse, "So fucking beautiful, Lydia." Once I fully (and somewhat reluctantly) pull away from her lips, I move to kiss down, down, down her neck and to the valley between her tits. My tongue circles her nipple, and I take it into my mouth fully without warning. Lydia gasps and reaches for me, tangling her fingers in my hair and tugging my curls in the most exquisite way, egging me on. After a few more needy licks and sucks, my eyes staying locked on hers, I pull away with a satisfying little pop and continue to kiss down her belly.

Then, when I reach the waistband of her pants, she reaches down with her free hand, unbuttoning and un-zipping her jeans almost torturously slowly. The look in her eyes tells me she knows what she's doing, she knows that she is teasing me to no end; I must be salivating by the time that she finally pushes her jeans and underwear down past her hips. I'm on my knees in front of her, gaze dark and resolute and full of nothing but pure lust as I watch her little show, noticing the glistening little spot of wetness that's left on her underwear as she kicks the last of her clothes to the floor.

"Jesus," I breathe, "You're so wet for me." I bend down again to start another trail of slow kisses towards her center, starting this time at her knee.

"Only for you," Lydia says through a moan, and I groan against her skin. Only for me. The idea of this threatens to go to my head, but I shake it off quickly, refocusing on the task at hand. My lips linger on the inside of her upper thigh as I let one of my hands trail up her other leg, dragging a finger along her slick folds and eliciting a gasp from her. My expression turns into a grin as I start to circle her clit ever so slowly with my middle finger, applying the lightest amount of pressure and relishing in the little gasps she makes with each small movement.

"Oh my God," She bucks her hips down into my hands a bit then, legs shaking, "Beck, please."

Her pleading is the thing that finally makes my resolve snap. I'm too full of want to tease her any further, and so without hesitation, I slip my finger inside of her warm and wet center, bending down so that my lips and my tongue can join in the effort. Lydia lets out a cry that almost sounds pained as I lick and suck at her clit, adding a second finger to curl and pump in and out of her. She tastes like nothing I've ever had before, and now that I've gotten a try of her, I know that I am never going to want to go back to the way things were before. I eat her out like my life depends on it, and she doesn't hold back, tugging my hair and panting out little affirmations and needy whines. Then, I feel her clenching around my fingers, and I hum softly against her skin, egging her on.

"Close," She breathes, forcing herself to look down at me, "Beck, I'm close. Oh, fuck." Lydia bites her bottom lip and looks like she's going to scream at any second. I don't change a thing — I don't pick up my pace or change my rhythm or stop the messy movements of my tongue. The stimulation of it all is exactly where she wants it, and I can tell. As I let out another groan of pleasure into her skin, her breathing quickens, gasping and moaning and throwing her head back.

"Beck!" She screams, then, and she falls apart all over my fingers and my face. The rhythmic clenching of her walls around me and the moans and cries of pleasure as she shakes are the sexiest things I've ever seen, and I have to stop myself from reaching down to start jacking off to the sight of it.

"God. Holy fuck, Lydia," I nearly growl as I continue to work her through her high, before her thighs clasp around my head. I don't want to stop, but I also don't want her to be overstimulated, so when she starts to pull away, I oblige, bringing my fingers to my lips and sucking the rest of her slick off them. For a moment, she's still, eyes closed and panting as she lays on my bed. I start to force myself to be content with it, to let her rest after getting her off and resign myself to getting myself off in the bathroom, but then she opens her eyes into mine, and they're just as full of lust as they were when we started.

"Beck, I want you. All of you. Please, please fuck me."

Chapter 7

Lydia

I don't know what I expected when I said it. When I asked him to give me everything. But Beck descends upon me like a man starved, like there has never been anything he's wanted more in his life. I find myself helpless against him, keening pathetically for him with need, and I know that how turned on I am for him has to be *so* obvious before he even starts to eat me out. But then he does, and it's all I can do not to scream. I don't know if it's the fact that I've been deprived of this kind of physical affection or the fact that it's *Beck*, but it's easily the most turned on I've ever been. It could also be the alcohol, but I'm more inclined to think it's one of the other two. That, or how forbidden it feels, how off limits that Beck seems to be.

I'm barely able to recover from reaching my peak before I feel his strong arms around me again, lifting me up and placing me further up on the bed than I had been before. As he hovers over the top of me, I can't help myself, so I slide my hand down below the waistband of his boxers, gasping as I wrap my hand around his length.

"Oh," I gasp, a bit shocked by the sheer size of it. It's so big, so thick and long that I have no idea how I'm going to be able to fit it in my mouth, let alone take it inside of me. Beck must take notice of my apprehension (that, or he's used to people finding his cock to be rather large), because once I take even the slightest notice of how completely huge he is, he chimes in again.

"You can take it, baby." His voice is coarse and needy, and I squeeze his length and pump him slowly as I marvel at his certainty. Even at the slightest touch, Beck groans deliciously, letting his hips rock into my hands. I've already finished once, but if I can tell anything about Beck, about how I *know* that he is going to fill me up so completely, it's that I'll without a doubt be finishing again. And this time, it'll be around his cock.

"Take these off," I finally order breathlessly, tugging at the waistband of his boxers as I move my wrist, slowly pumping his length before I run my thumb across the soft tip delicately. "Now." Beck moans again, louder this time, and he does what he's told, pulling away from me for a moment to finally free himself completely from his clothes. His pupils are blown, and his eyes are wild, with a gaze that seems to threaten that he's going to pounce at any moment.

"Oh God, look at you..." He mumbles, crawling back up to me and capturing my lips for another open-mouthed kiss, "You're so fucking perfect, Lydia." His words and the conviction with which he says them sends a chill through me, my back arching up involuntarily as I feel his hands start to roam down my body again, before they land on my hips. Beck lifts up my hips slightly, then, before lining himself up with my entrance, teasing it a bit with his tip. I whine pathetically, fingertips digging into his shoulders.

"You ready?" He asks, through gritted teeth. But his face falls for a moment, and I furrow my eyebrows. "Ah, shit. Do we need a condom—"

"Yeah," I say breathlessly, and I'm grateful that Beck is able to produce one from his bedside drawer. I watch as he rips it open with his teeth, a bit mesmerized by how blatantly *sexy* it is to see him doing something like that, even though it is nearly animalistic. He hands me the condom, and I roll it onto his length, grinning up at him as he clenches his jaw and moans at the feeling of my hands on him again.

"Okay," I breathe, moving him to line back up with me. "I'm ready."

Then, without hesitation, Beck starts to push in — I was right, he is deliciously huge, and I let out a sharp gasp followed by a cry that's a mix of pain and pleasure. I feel tears starting to sting my eyes, but the burn of the stretching of my walls is so lovely that I dig my heels in below his ass, willing him to push himself in further.

"Easy, now," Beck says gently, a low chuckle leaving his lips. "I know you want it, and you *can* take it, but you need to give yourself a minute to adjust first, okay? I don't want you to overdo it." Begrudgingly, I nod, but even still, I want to wiggle myself down, rutting my hips into his and impale myself on him, letting him fill me completely. I'm so needy for him that it threatens to consume me.

His thrusts are slow, at first. He's gentle, allowing me the time that I need to get used to the sheer size of him. But once my tight walls finally loosen up enough and he slips all the way in, I basically yell his name, feeling so full and *content* that I could almost sob. I've never felt so stretched, so utterly *had* by someone that just the feeling of even the smallest of thrusts threatens to make me fall apart.

"More," I gasp, fingernails digging into his skin as I brace myself on his shoulders. Beck finally obliges, letting himself start to thrust into me with a steadily increasing amount of vigor. My eyes fall closed as I let myself go, let myself feel every single one of his movements, relishing in the expertise of his attentions with me. I could do this with him forever, I think, could let myself fall over and over again into his bed, into these sheets, his willing accomplice in this act of sin and pleasure for the rest of my life.

"Oh God, Lydia," He gasps, moving to press down on me even further, letting his full weight press me down into the mattress. He's so huge, not just his dick, but just *him* — he's become such a huge and imposing man that I almost don't recognize him. The thick carpeting of hair across his chest fully proves it, that Beck is a *man*, where before I must have only been with boys, concerned only for their own pleasure.

"Lydia, honey, look at me. Open your eyes." I'm almost too enraptured in him, in my own pleasure to hear him, but somehow, the sweetness with which he says my name breaks through the haze of my desire, and I oblige, his baby blues meeting my hazel irises.

The electricity between us is taut, pulsating. His open mouth ghosts over mine, our breath mingling as he picks up the pace, pinning one of his hands right at the side of my head. The other hand that had before been firmly situated on my hip moves, then, beginning to work circles into my clit. It's almost too much, almost *too* good, and I cry out helplessly, completely at his mercy. My climax starts to build again, then, and I'm so willing to give in to him, so willing to give him every single bit of me.

"Close," I manage through a gasp, my lips brushing against his as I speak. "Fuck, Beck, oh my God. I'm going to—"

"Come for me, baby. I need to feel you," He rasps, and his pace picks up slightly, his breathing ragged. I know that he's close too, the little moans and gasps falling from his lips increasing in frequency. Then, he hits that spot, just *there* inside me, and the pleasure of it combined with the feeling of his fingers on my clit does it for me, sending me over the edge for the second time that night.

"Beck!" I cry, back arching off the bed as my hands fly into his hair, tugging at his blonde curls. He lets out a grunt and another shaky moan as he finishes, his thrusts slow and deliciously hard as he works himself through his own high. Then, he stills inside me, his eyes falling shut as he collapses on top of me fully. The little ringlets of his hair are plastered to his forehead with sweat, his lips red and parted and swollen, and he looks so much like that little boy I used to race off the dock every summer that my fondness for him threatens to swallow me whole. I can't help myself — I push them off his forehead so delicately, before I let my arms embrace him fully, holding him tight like he would evaporate if I didn't.

In that moment, I come to the startling realization that I could *love* him, if I wasn't careful. That if I let myself, I could slip fully into the hedge maze of his affections, and I could get lost in him.

I banish these thoughts from my mind entirely as I hold him, though, my willingness to just let myself *be* winning out over my tendency to overthink for once. And I slip fully into oblivion, with Beck Shepherd as my only anchor.

Chapter 8

Lydia

After that night at Callaghan's (and the events there-after), Beck and I don't talk much. On paper, at least, we pretend like the second half of that night never happened. I was *absolutely* not going to be the one who brought it up first, and Beck didn't seem to feel like unpacking "what it meant" either, so our conversations have mostly focused on trip logistics for the past two weeks, which has been fine with me. There was plenty to plan, anyways, and I'd become an expert at avoiding difficult conversations thanks to my shitty marriage, so it was really a win-win situation for me.

I don't know if I would even call it a win, though. It's more like a flimsy success that hinges entirely on my ability to make sure that things stay wholly un-awkward for the entirety of the trip. *Should be easy, right?* I try to convince myself, repeating it over and over like a mantra in my head as I pack one of my suitcases. *I mean, it's*

Beck, *your childhood best friend. Beck, who you've known for the majority of your life. Beck, who you... who you had sex with two weeks ago after three years of not talking.*

Oh God, this is going to be a disaster.

I know by this point, though, that it's too late to back out. That I'm pretty much doomed for whatever awkward and inevitable fate that I'm barreling straight towards, full steam ahead. There's no stopping it, and maybe there wasn't any in the first place. Maybe it was always going to end up like this, with me alone and confused over my best friend of 25 years, trying to fit two weeks' worth of clothes into two tiny suitcases to save myself money on a checked bag for our flight.

As I'm mentally sorting through my checklist, though, listing off all of the essentials in my head — *phone charger, toothbrush, deodorant* — I'm struck with the idea of the new reality that I might need to face. Once I'm in my bathroom, sorting through all of the essentials, I catch a glimpse of the box of condoms that I always keep, my *just in case* stash. I've always been of the opinion that it's better for me to be safe than sorry, and I don't know why this wouldn't apply now, especially considering the... new *development* in my friendship with Beck. So, I grab the box, taking it into my room quickly as I try to consider the most efficient way to pack them.

Eventually, I decide that the box isn't going to fit in either my checked bag *or* my carry on, and so I make the executive decision to simply empty the box into my carry on, a few loose condoms falling on top of my underwear, the rest still connected to one another in long strips.

But, as if on cue, I hear Amber's voice echoing down the hallway, calling out my name in her sing-songy voice. Panic floods me, and I try to shut my bag, so she doesn't see, but the zipper snags. So, against my better judgment, I grab as many of the condoms as I can, trying to hide them behind my back.

I'm too late, though. Amber opens the door without knocking, and I'm standing there, clutching two handfuls of condoms, my cheeks heating and coloring. We stared at each other for a long beat, a puzzled look on her face.

"This isn't what it looks like!" I stammer out finally, breaking the silence between the two of us as a couple of the condoms slip from my grip, clattering awkwardly to the ground.

"Lydia, what?" Amber laughs, blinking rapidly as she watches my clear exasperation. "I didn't even say anything—"

"They're for Greece!" I insist, my voice too loud and my pitch too high. I bend over to pick up the dropped condoms, shoving them back into my bag as quickly as I can manage.

"What if I meet a man in Greece? I mean, it's never a *bad* thing to be too prepared—"

"Oh my *God*, Dee, I literally didn't even ask a *single* question about it."

"I'm just—"

"I mean, what do you want me to do?" She asks, laughing at my expense as she watches me struggle again with my zipper, "Ask if you're planning to sleep with my brother or something?" The words make me color even further; I have never been good at lying, especially not to Amber. She's like a second sister to me, and the guilt of lying to her mingles with my embarrassment, making me feel unsteady.

"Lalalalalalala! I can't hear you!" I say, covering my ears childishly, trying to convey a sense that even the *thought* of Beck in a sensual manner is something that would never cross my mind. Her words make me color even further, though; I have never been good at lying, especially not to Amber. She's like a second sister to me, and the guilt of lying to her mingles with my embarrassment, making me feel unsteady. "Aaaaaah, if I can't hear you then what you're saying is irrelevant—"

"Jesus! Okay! I'm just glad you're not going to get a disease from a foreign man or whatever, I just wanted to see if you needed any help with your packing—"

"I've got it covered!" I chirp, trying my best to sound convincing as I cross the room to her, stepping out of my room as I place both of my hands on her shoulders. I don't know when or if I will ever tell her about what happened between Beck and I, but right before a trip that she paid for *definitely* doesn't seem like the most opportune moment. So, I take a deep breath, trying to steady myself as I look at her. "But hey, thank you again — for everything. Really, Amber, I mean it. This whole thing... It's a dream. I only wish that I could repay you somehow." Amber smiles at me, then, and pulls me into a tight hug.

"You can *repay* me by having the time of your life. Oh, and you have to promise me that you'll take lots of pictures, so I can live vicariously through you." We laugh as she pulls away, and I try not to let the guilt of not telling her everything then and there eat me alive. *It's not technically a lie, though*, I tell myself, *you're not planning to sleep with Beck again. It's more of an omission than anything, and what she doesn't know won't hurt her.*

If that's the case, though, why do I still feel so ashamed?

***

Three days later, I'm awake at 5:00 AM on a Saturday morning, only slightly miserable with the relative lack of sleep. Beck and I had agreed to get to the airport early, though, and I'm thankful that he shares my propensity for being a healthy amount of overprepared. Even despite the early hour, DC's Reagan National Airport is still almost heinously crowded, and I wonder where on Earth all of these people have come from, or where they need to go so early.

But, then again, I know that they could likely be thinking the exact same thing about me. Airports have always been such a strange reminder for me that the world is a much bigger place than I realize, and that every single person going from place to place has a life that is as rich and as complex as mine.

But, then again, it's too early for me to be thinking about things that are so philosophical.

Once I say goodbye to Amber, I make my way straight to the bag check station, where Beck and I had decided to meet. I spot him easily, his tall frame towering over the crowd around him. I tend to forget how tall being six foot four inches actually is in comparison to the rest of the world, particularly since it's *Beck*, who I was solidly taller than for at least three summers when we were in middle school. He smiles at me, then, clearly having seen me at the same time, waving me over to him. I snake my way through the crowd, the fluorescent light reflecting off the floor in a way that I am *positive* is deeply unflattering to me and to the rest of the human race who are forced to be in a place like this so early. Once I finally reach Beck, though, I'm dismayed to find that he somehow looks *gorgeous*, even this early, and I mentally kick myself for thinking such a thing.

"Hey there, pal," He says once I reach him, with heavy emphasis on the word 'pal'. I have to fight back the desire to cringe at this, deflating slightly at how it feels to be called a friendly nickname by him. Just a couple of weeks ago, I was *honey* and *baby* when I was in his arms. I try to quickly shake off the disappointment; *You're not his, Lydia. You're just friends.*

"Hey, Beck," I say, and he extends his arm to me, wrapping me up in probably one of the most awkward side hugs of all time. I can't help but feel like I'm a kid at a youth camp who can't be seen touching a boy for longer than five seconds without getting in trouble when he touches me like this. It almost makes me want to crawl out of my skin, so I break the hug first, looking up at him with a tight smile. He smiles back, and it almost seems easier for him, much to my dismay. *Jerk. Can he just sleep around and not care?* Immediately, I chastise myself for this line of thinking. It is just Beck, after all. I have no idea what he could be thinking.

"So, you ready for this?" he finally asks, hoisting our checked bags onto the table in front of us. "Honestly, it's been a few years since I've been to the summer house."

"Oh yeah?" I ask, grateful for the turn of conversation. "When was the last time you went?"

"With Heather." Another long pause passes between us at the mention of his late wife. I know that I'm giving him a pitying look, because he laughs in spite of himself, rubbing the back of his neck as we receive our receipts for baggage claim. "Wow, we're off to a great start," he says with a sigh, and we step away from the desk, headed towards the security line. I'm thankful to see that it's not as long as I had expected, and I pat his shoulder reassuringly before I speak, trying hard not to overthink this extra physical contact.

"It's fine," I say, "I know that it's probably really hard for you. I know... I know that place was special to you guys." He nods at me, and I can see the grief in his eyes, the brief glint of a deep and pervasive sadness that clouds his thinking. And then, I have a thought that fills me with so much guilt that it almost swallows me up. *It was our place first.* I think about it before I can stop myself, and I feel nauseous at how selfish that I could be. That house was the place where they got engaged, where they had built so many memories as a young family.

But it was special to *us*, too.

It's silent for the entire time that we go through security, the things unsaid stretching taut between us. I don't know how to cope with it, with the unrelenting itch that comes with how... deeply *awkward* it all is. I feel like I could break out into hives at any moment. My throat is dry, and I barely notice it when we're finally past the checkpoint, walking alongside each other past the gates in a mechanical silence.

I hate this. I *hate* it, and I refuse for my entire vacation to go this way. We have to get past this, we *have* to. There's too much history for us to not.

"Hey, okay," I blurt out finally, grabbing his arm, stopping him in the middle of the walkway. He turns to me, brow furrowed, clearly puzzled by how suddenly it is that I'm stopping him. "I can't take this anymore. We fucked. So what?" I realize far too late that I'm talking *entirely* too loudly. An old couple walks by us, a look of pure shock on the woman's face. Beck catches her eye and reddens all the way to his ears, giving me a pleading look. I pull him closer, then, lowering my voice before I continue.

"We fucked. And it was good," I say to him, voice barely above a whisper, "That's *it*. Nothing else has to happen. There doesn't have to be all this... this *weirdness* about it. We're adults. It happened. We can either acknowledge it and move on and agree to not be careless like that again or we can let this ruin our vacation. And I don't know about you, but I *need* this vacation. So do we have a deal?"

Beck searches my eyes, chewing on the inside of his cheek. He's quiet for almost *too* long of a moment before he finally nods definitively, extending his hand to me.

"Yeah, okay. Deal." I shake his hand, and for a moment, we're two kids again, making a bet on who can eat the most ice cream without getting brain freeze. "Although, I gotta say it— this feels like a really weird sex pact."

"What?" I say, a laugh bubbling past my lips, a surge of relief washing over me. "How is it a sex pact? What even *is* a sex pact? We literally just agreed we were going to move on."

"Stop saying 'sex pact' so loud."

"You said it first!" Beck sticks his tongue out at me, and I do the same — suddenly, we're just kids again, laughing at one another's antics.

"A sex pact would be like... a pact you make to lose your virginity to someone if you both haven't lost it by a certain time. Kind of like a marriage pact. So, this would be, like, the opposite. Kind of."

"You just made all of that up. You're so weird."

"Pot, kettle."

"Whatever, Shepherd. I need a drink."

We end up in the airport bar after that, deciding to have a couple of mimosas with our breakfast (because it seems to be the only thing that's appropriate to drink in the morning). What I don't anticipate, though, is how potent the alcohol in just one mimosa seems to be. Typically, they don't affect me like this, but without having breakfast beforehand, I have severely underestimated my tolerance, and I'm tipsy before I even realize it. I can't complain about it though, because I do have a very minor fear of flying, so the slight buzz takes the edge off.

Once we leave the bar, we wait for a while at the gate, entertaining ourselves by people watching and discussing our observations. We take turns making up life stories for each of the people around us, deciding that a couple who looked like they'd been married for quite some time were going to visit one of their children and that a group of girls were going on a bachelorette trip (that one, though, was a bit more obvious — one of the girls *did* have on a sash that said "wife of the party", so we didn't really have to work too hard to come to that conclusion). The time goes by relatively quickly, though, and we're boarding the flight before we know it, taking off without incident.

"Is it bad luck if I say, 'I hope we don't die' after the airplane takes off?" I ask Beck once the fasten seatbelts sign turns off, drumming my fingertips against the arm rest.

"I feel like it certainly can't be good," He mutters, his attention rather squarely focused on the book that he's reading.

"Wait, oh crap," I say, my eyes widening; I'm definitely still feeling the alcohol, and I think that it may be clouding my judgment, because I grab Beck's forearm playfully as I speak.

"Did I jinx us? I shouldn't have said anything out loud—"

"Dude, it's fine," Beck chuckles, his eyes darting from my hand on his arm up to my face. "Just relax. Here." Then, he pokes his head out into the aisle, flagging down one of the flight attendants with a wave. "Excuse me, could we get two mimosas, please?"

"Oh, you trying to get me drunk again?" I squeeze his arm as I say this, a sly smile on my face. "Remember what happened *last* time—"

"Actually, make that two mimosas and a shot of tequila."

"Wow, didn't expect you to be so blatant about it—"

"It's for me, you dork."

"Am I that hard to deal with?"

"Yes."

"Wow," I breathe, feigning incredulousness, "Over twenty years of friendship and me putting out and *this* is the thanks I get?"

"Have you no shame, woman?" He laughs, "The entire plane can probably hear you talking about putting out."

I wave off his concern, shaking my head as I notice the flight attendant coming back with our drinks.

"I'll never see any of these people ever again," I shrug, and Beck gives me a knowing nod. I hold up my drink in his direction, then, tipping my glass towards his. "Beck, I would like to propose a toast."

"Okay?" He raises an eyebrow at me, but tilts his drink towards mine, nonetheless.

"To what could potentially be the most awkward trip of all time. May we, in fact, *not* let it be awkward and instead have a good time in spite of the fact that we may have just fundamentally altered our friendship forever after having drunk sex."

Beck laughs heartily. "Hear, hear." Then, we touch our glasses together, and I can't help but think about what happened after the last time we had a toast.

The rest of the flight is uneventful. We mostly just read our books or have conversations about what our favorite vacations of the past were. I spend a lot of time looking out the window, staring at the world below; everything looks so small from up here, and I'm reminded of how small *I* really must be in the scheme of things, how insignificant my life must be. But, just as soon as I'm about to get a little bit *too* existential, I hear the pilot announce that we're beginning our descent into Florida.

When we land, Beck is very efficient in making sure that we have all of our carry-ons and getting us off the crowded plane in a timely manner. Baggage claim doesn't take us too long either, thankfully, but the one thing that's bothering me the most is how dry my lips feel from being in the air locked cabin at such a high altitude. We meet the driver who's taking us down to the cape outside the airport (her name is Janice, and she's very heavily tattooed), and as we're loading our things in the trunk, I decide to try and find my chapstick that was in my carry on.

What I neglect to realize, though, is that I somehow managed to bury my Chapstick at the very bottom of the bag. And that some of the stuff must have gotten knocked around with all of the movement. I unzip my bag, and condoms come flying out of it, landing all over the back of the car and at my feet.

"Oh, holy shit. Okay," I manage, my face going red hot with embarrassment as I try to shove them back inside the bag. The color on my face only deepens as I hear Beck stifling a laugh behind me.

"Woah. So, we're *forgetting* about it, huh?" He says through his laughter, and I give him a harsh look once I've hidden all the evidence, returning to his side.

"Oh, nothing to worry about!" Janice says then, her hands gesturing wildly as she speaks. "I promise y'all, I've driven plenty of honeymooners before. And I can just tell by the way you're embarrassed that you're not going to be getting up to anything in the back seat like some of the others did—"

"No, oh God, no," I stammer, lifting up my hands in an apologetic stance, "I mean, we're not—"

"Trust us, we'll save it all for when we're in private," Beck starts, cutting my thought short as he throws his arm around me confidently, smiling down at me before pressing a long kiss to my cheek. If I wasn't blushing before, I am now — my face feels hot, and I swallow harshly. *What is he* doing? "My new wife, here, would probably appreciate it if this didn't remain the topic of conversation, though." He gives me a look, then, a raise of the eyebrows that clearly says *go along with it*. I must look puzzled, because he leans in closer to me, pecking my cheek a second time and whispering, "Trust me."

"Understood," Janice says with a wink, and she gestures for us to follow her as we climb into the back seat of the black SUV.

It isn't too long of a drive before we arrive at the beach house, and it's exactly how I remember it. Seashore Way is a side street full of brightly colored houses that backs up directly to the beach, with the Shepherd family home situated right on the cul-de-sac. It's the same buttery yellow that I remember on the outside, but with a fresh coat of paint, lifted up on stilts similarly to the other surrounding houses. Immediately, I'm hit with a wave of nostalgia, of memories of going to Beck and Amber's dock on the bay side of the cape, of taking out their boat and spending the day in the sun until we were nearly exhausted. We unpack and we tip Janice in cash, giving her twice the amount we usually would since she gave us half off the ride as a wedding present.

"Are we terrible people for lying to that lady about us being married?" I ask, grabbing my bags and starting up the stairs to the porch, "Jesus, I feel terrible."

"You shouldn't," Beck reassures me, "She didn't lose out on anything, it's the corporation she works for that did. If anything, we probably just gave her the best payday she's had in a little while since we tipped her in cash. Oh, and her score will go up for the glowing review I just left, so it's a win for everyone involved."

"I guess you're right," I say, huffing slightly once I finally reach the landing.

"So, are we going to talk about the condoms...?"

"Don't even *think* about it, Shepherd," I hold up my hand to stop him, "It's merely a precaution."

"A precaution."

"Yes, for Greece."

"Greece?"

"Yeah, what if I meet someone over there?" Saying this makes me feel deeply guilty for some reason that I can't place. I feel so *bad* for making him think that this might be my intention, but I try to swallow these feelings, avoiding his eyes as he finally opens the door, ushering me inside.

"I see."

"If you're nice, I might let you borrow one."

"Gee, how thoughtful."

"Oh, shut up."

Chapter 9

Beck

Once we've unpacked, I lay in my childhood bedroom and look up at the ceiling fan, watching it spin as I let my mind wander. Most of the house has gotten updated, but Amber and I's bedrooms have stayed relatively untouched — it's almost like stepping into a time capsule. Lydia's staying in Amber's room, which connects to mine through a shared bathroom. My walls, once painted blue, are covered in posters from movies that I loved or bands that I listened to back in high school. I remember, then, the summer that Lydia and I turned 16. I'd known that Lydia was beautiful from the first time I even *thought* about looking at a girl in that way, but there was something about how she really came into herself that year that cemented it for me.

And without even really trying, I'm suddenly a teenager again, helplessly in love with the girl who's also my best friend.

Just then, there's a knock on my bedroom door, and Lydia pokes her head inside before I can even answer.

"Hey, you hungry? Because I, for one, am starving, and would probably commit a laundry list of crimes to go to Craig's right about now." Just the thought of the raw bar that's the staple of the town makes my mouth water, and I'm standing up before I can even verbally agree. "Starving. Let's go."

***

"Honestly, I don't know why our parents and the entirety of this town decided to trust an oyster bar called Crabby Craig's, but I'm glad that they did," Lydia says definitively once we're seated at a high top table inside the restaurant, "This place is an institution."

"Thirty years later and it's still just as questionable as when they started out, but man, if the food isn't good." It's also only a six-minute drive away from the house, which has always been a plus, particularly on nights when no one really felt like cooking.

"I mean, honestly, if you're going to eat at an oyster bar and it *doesn't* look like there might be something sticky on the floor, then you're in the wrong place."

"But the floors are never sticky."

"Oh, exactly, it's very clean, but it's the aesthetic that matters. You get all of the vibes of the filth but none of the food poisoning." She's right about this — the place is small and dimly-lit, with wooden tables and chairs that look as though they might have been around since the 90's. The menus, cheaply laminated and falling apart, are tucked into the napkin tray, and the walls are scarcely visible for the dollar bills that have been stapled on every available surface.

Each one has something written on it too, classic catchphrases like "Chuck and Becky 4Ever",

"Buy the bride a drink! @Zoebrooke4347 on Venmo", and "The birds work for the government".

"And, since it's only the aesthetic that's unclean, you'll only throw up from drinking too much beer rather than from eating bad shellfish."

Lydia cringes at this but laughs all the same. "Maybe we shouldn't be talking about this right before we eat."

"Yeah, that's... yeah."

Our waitress, Reina, approaches the table then. She looks like she can't possibly be over five feet tall, but her deeply tanned skin and bleach blonde hair let me know that she is a Florida native through and through. That, and the tattoo she has on her forearm that says "hold my beer". I would put money on the fact that she's probably wrestled an alligator before. She takes our drink order first and disappears behind the bar swiftly afterwards.

"Why do I feel like that woman would probably fight a bear and win?" Lydia asks once she walks away, voice hushed slightly. I have to stifle a laugh — even though we didn't think the exact same thing, we still had the same train of thought, which makes me laugh all the more.

"Because she's busy running this place like the Navy. Look," I point towards the back of the room, where she's grabbing our drinks while simultaneously directing the busboys towards which tables to clean. "I recognize her, she's been here for nearly a decade, it seems. She's the manager now. Has been for like, five years, I think? But she also refuses to stop waiting tables."

"Reina's like a shark. If she stops moving, she dies." Lydia looks fascinated, and I chuckle again as our drinks are brought to our table.

"Reina is my hero," I say solemnly, raising up my beer as proof of this, before taking a swig.

"You know who my hero probably is?" Lydia muses, swirling the straw around in her margarita.

"Who?"

"Ryan Gosling."

I quirk my eyebrow in surprise. "Okay, elaborate."

"Well, I mean, just — okay, look at his career trajectory. After doing that one movie, Blue Valentine, I think? Well, that movie messed with his head. And he was so open about it, like, talking about it publicly, and he said he would never do something like that again because he absolutely *refused* to put his family through it. So now he's taking all of these strictly comedic roles and only wants to do things that he thinks are fun. He was so perfect in *Barbie*. I just respect him so much for how open he was about all of that and for the way he puts his family first. It gives me hope that maybe men aren't all bad."

She has a point, and I nod along with her, taking another sip of my beer. "He should have won an Oscar for *La La Land*."

"Thank you! Yes, he should have won an Oscar for *La La Land*."

"I don't even remember who won Best Actor that year. He was definitely nominated."

"He's *never* won. It's a crime!" She says it with such conviction that we're both laughing.

It seems like the laughter isn't going to slow any time soon, which I don't mind in the slightest. But, there are some things that I think we definitely need to clear the air on, and if we don't talk about it now, I'm worried that there won't be another good time before we're really in the thick of the trip. And I'd rather cover the hard stuff now and have our fun later.

"So. I'm..." I start, and a pause passes between us. "Listen, I'm sorry if this is too forward, but all this talk about... good husbands? What happened with you and Tristan?"

Lydia studies me for a moment, before letting out a long sigh. "I mean, it's been years of stuff, really." She casts her gaze downward, and I notice that she's picking at her nails underneath the table as she speaks. "It all just kind of... piled up. I've always been really career driven, and Tristan was fine with it, at first. Or at least he said he was. And, I mean, when we first started dating, he and I... we partied a lot, which was also fine. But we were young, it was what we were supposed to be doing.

But Tristan just... he never really slowed down. He would get mad at me when I wouldn't go out with him because I had worked the next morning, which... He drank alone a lot. And then he started to drink after work most days and came home later and later. Then he'd insist that *I* was the one who had the problem of staying late at work doing things to try to get promoted instead of staying home and cooking or cleaning or doing the laundry. And I realized, one day, that I didn't want someone like him to be the father of my kids.

 So that was just... that was it."

Lydia pauses again, and I notice that she's trying to fight back tears. But I don't say anything — I just reach across the table and squeeze her hand as she continues. "We got into this big fight about it, and he tried to apologize, but when I brought up the fact that he had *never* bought me flowers, not even once, I realized that he had never even bothered to learn what my favorite flower *was*."

"Violets," I say, without hesitation. Lydia blinks several times, her eyes meeting mine again, a look that I can't read on her face.

"... What?" The tiniest smile appears on her lips, and I kick myself a little for being so forward with my memory of these small details about her.

"I mean, uh, you —" I stammer, clearing my throat. "Mom always grew violets. In her flower beds. You've loved them since you were a kid, and she would always make you these tiny little bouquets of them. Violets are your favorite."

"Oh." A pause stretches between us. "I didn't know that you remembered that."

"I remember everything about you, Dee."

Lydia looks at me, *really* looks at me then, and I take note of the color tinting her cheeks.

Pride swells in my chest — I won't ever tire of being able to get a reaction out of her.

"Well," she says simply, before taking a sip of her drink to break some of the tension.

"Anyways, now it's your turn to spill your guts. How have you been? Since... since Heather?"

"Right." I probably should have seen this question coming, but I cast my own gaze down now all the same. "I've been... I've been doing about as well as you could expect. Questioning what I'm doing with my life, waxing poetic over my dead-end job, picking up pottery as a hobby to try to find some meaning in an otherwise meaningless existence."

"Pottery? You've been doing pottery?"

"Yeah, I go pretty much every week to this studio near my apartment. I just... it's really soothing, the mechanics of it all. The wheel is so smooth and it's very calming. And the idea of creating something out of nothing? That I made a bowl or a vase or a teapot out of clay that was completely formless beforehand? It all just... it makes me feel like I have a purpose beyond being just another person wasting their life behind a computer at a desk job."

"That's how travel has always made me feel," she says, and I can tell that it's genuine, that she *really* understands the passion that I have for this. "The world is so amazing. I think I've always seen my job as a bit of a means to an end, you know? If I do what I need to do, then I can see corners of the world that I've only ever dreamed of."

"Oh, come on, you don't like your job? You've idolized Elle Woods since we were teenagers."

"Well, *yeah*," She scoffs, but I take note of the teasing smile on her face, "But just because I enjoy my job and am good at it doesn't mean it's what I *love*. I actually... I *hate* confrontation. I hate arguing. That part of the law makes me want to crawl out of my skin. What I really love about it is that I almost never stop learning, never stop studying. It's always a challenge, and I love a good challenge. But my heart? My true love? That's traveling." There's a sparkle in Lydia's eyes when she says this, one that I don't think I've seen in about three years. I would do anything, give absolutely *anything* to preserve it. I'm still holding her hand, I notice, and I give it another squeeze, the feeling of her fingers laced through mine grounding me.

"I'm glad I get to experience this with you, then. A place you've never been before. I feel very lucky to."

The tension stretches taut between us as I grin across the table at her, and we sit there like that, letting ourselves live in it for just a moment. The electricity that courses through me is undeniable as she lets her thumb trace against the skin of my hand gently, and all I want, all I *need* is more.

If I wasn't already in trouble, I most *certainly* am now.

Chapter 10

Lydia

After we got back from dinner, I lay on the bottom bunk of the bed that used to be Amber's and stared listlessly up at the beams holding up the top mattress. My heart still feels like it's about to beat out of my chest. What is *happening?* Why is there still so much tension between Beck and me? I replay it over and over again in my head, trying to remember how it felt to have his hands on me *without* making it something romantic, but I just can't detach the idea now.

It has already lodged itself there, taking root and threatening to cover me completely like ivy.

I remember how excited Amber; Liv and I had been when the Shepherds bought this bed for us. After a few years of all three of us managing to squeeze ourselves into the full-size bed that was here previously, it felt like Christmas had come early. A bunk bed with two full size mattresses. The three of us always used to fight over who would get the top bunk until my mom made us start a rotation. I now assume this was more for her sanity than for a lesson in sharing between three preteen girls, but we kept up with it religiously, always remembering whose turn it would be the first night of the next vacation based on who slept on the top bunk last.

I tried to climb up there, when Beck and I first arrived, for nostalgia purposes. But getting up there was *significantly* harder than I remember it being. Either that, or I'm just getting old, but my melancholy is only interrupted when I realize that I'll probably hit my head on the top bunk at least once on this vacation, knowing my luck.

My tangential thoughts about my childhood memories in this house are inextricably linked with Beck, though, and even during my little trip down memory lane, my mind finds its way back to him. I try in vain to journal but find that the words that usually come so easily to me when I'm writing about my trips have completely abandoned me. I am hopeless. If I don't get this off my chest in some way other than on paper, I think I'll probably spontaneously combust.

Olivia. I need Olivia. I need my big sister.

When I call her, she answers on the first ring.

"Dee, hey! How's the vacation?" She chirps, and the words are spilling out of my mouth before I can stop them.

"Beck and I slept together." I hear the sound of something clattering to the floor on the other line.

"Wait, *what* did you just say?"

"We slept together," I repeat, letting out a sigh of relief. Finally, someone knows. "I don't know what happened. I don't know *how* it happened."

"When? Last night? Oh my *God*, Dee!"

"Keep it down!" The pitch of my sister's voice can sometimes reach astronomically ear-splitting new heights. This is one of those times.

"Chill, no one can hear me! Answer my question!"

"No, it wasn't last night. It was... it was the night after I moved in with Amber and Melanie."

"What? Holy shit! Why didn't you tell me?" Olivia's tone lands somewhere between excited and accusatory.

"Because I didn't know how to. I didn't know... I didn't know what to do. I didn't tell anyone." Static crackles between our phones. She is silent for a moment, and I picture her making the face that she makes when she's thinking really hard. The face she used to make when she was studying in high school.

"Well? Was it good?" She says finally, and even though no one is in the room, I know that my cheeks are the color of a tomato.

"Liv, that is *so* not the point right now."

"But was it *good*, though?" My sister presses, and I flop back onto the bed in exasperation.

"Of course it was."

"That's so crazy! Not that I thought Beck would be bad or anything, I just—"

"Okay, that train of thought ends here."

"Sorry. So, wait, why did you wait so long to tell me?" she asks, her voice dropping to a whisper. "Did something else happen?"

"Yeah, kind of."

"Tell me everything."

So, I do. I tell her about how my entire world felt rocked after seeing him again for the first time in three years, how he makes me laugh harder than I have for as long as I can remember, how he looks at me in a way that simultaneously makes me feel seen *and* desired. That I feel like I could die when he touches my skin. I leave out all of the more intimate details, though, of course — I wouldn't want either of us to have to know *that* kind of thing about the other. Olivia is quiet for a moment after that, and the silence almost speaks for itself. I know how huge this all is, we *both* do. And as much as I'm trying to convince myself that this can just be something casual with Beck, I'm afraid that Olivia is going to tell me something that I'm not ready to hear; It can never be just casual with someone you're already that close with.

"Holy shit," She says, finally breaking the silence, "He's crazy about you."

"What?" I laugh, trying to sound surprised. Trying to sound like that very thought hadn't crossed my mind so many times over the last few weeks. "Okay, now you're the one who's joking."

"Dee, trust me. I run the most successful short romance publishing company in the business. I know this stuff. He's getting personal with you, sharing his emotions. There's physical contact. Oh, and not to mention the fact that he's quite obviously been in love with you for years."

"That's a stretch," I lie. "You can't know that." But she *can know* that, and she most likely does. She's right, though. Small and Sparkling has made her an expert on these matters, but there's nothing that will make a younger sister want to crawl out of their skin more than admitting that her older sister is right about something.

Olivia scoffs. "Anyone who's ever been within thirty feet of the two of you together knows that."

"Seriously?"

"Thomas even asked me if there was something going on between the two of you at Callaghan's that night. I, of course, told him no, but now I know that the proper answer would have been 'not yet'—"

"Okay, okay!" I say through clenched teeth, burying my face in a pillow. "I get it. Feel free to gloat or whatever, because I have no idea what to do."

"I'm not going to *gloat*. But are you enjoying yourself?"

"Of course I am," I sigh, voice muffled as I attempt to bury my face even further in my pillow. "How could I not be? He's gorgeous."

"Then just have fun. I mean, you said it yourself, you're both adults, so as long as you're on the same page about it all, who cares? Don't let me get in your head."

"Liv, I just got Beck back. I don't want to lose him again."

"You won't," she says decisively, and I can tell that she means it.

"How do you know?"

"Because I know he feels the exact same way about you. He's not letting you go again now that he has *you* back."

I don't know how to reconcile it all. I want to think that she's right, that he really did miss me all this time and that our friendship is strong enough to last even if everything that's happening between the two of us recently ends in chaos. But a little nagging thought at the back of my mind reminds me that he lived without me once. He would be more than capable of doing it again if things between the two of us got messy.

I'm about to try to explain all of this to Olivia when I hear my phone start to beep. Puzzled and wondering who could be calling in, I furrow my brow, only for my stomach to drop as soon as I see it.

It's Tristan.

My heart races. Immediately I'm anxious, and if I were on the phone with any other person, I would try to play it off. Would lie and say it was just one of my parents or a coworker or something that could be moderately convincing. But Olivia's on the other line, the person who knows me best. She would be able to see through the dishonesty immediately, and I've been silent for far too long at this point, trying to work out what to do.

"What?" I finally blurt out for lack of anything better to say, tuning back in to hear my sister rambling. Clearly,

I hadn't said anything for enough time to make her think that the call had dropped.

"Hello? Earth to Lydia?" She says, her voice taking on an impatient tone. "Can you hear me? I was just saying that Beck is obsessed with you—"

"Tristan is calling me." I interrupt her train of thought, but I probably couldn't have stopped myself if I tried. Anxiety rises into my chest, threatening to strangle me. I feel like I could throw up.

"Huh?" Olivia exclaims, clearly as shocked as I feel. "Hang up on him!"

"He hasn't called me in months. What if it's an emergency?" I chastise myself mentally to try to rationalize it.

"Tough cookies, he should have thought about that before he decided to be a Grade A asshole." The fact remains, though, that as soon as I saw his name appear on my phone, I knew I was going to answer. It's almost like a morbid curiosity, like whatever compels the main characters in horror movies to open the front door even when they *know* that there's danger outside.

It's self-destructive. But when someone was such a huge part of your life for so long, lines become blurred.

"Liv, it could be something serious," I say, "It could be his parents. I have to take this." My sister sighs, but I know that she'll let me be once I say this. Divorce is complicated. It's not like we'd just been dating and had a messy breakup — our lives had been completely and totally intertwined for so long and then violently severed apart. As badly as I wish I could just wave a magic wand and make all of the lingering complexities disappear, I know it's not that easy. "Okay," She says, "You can do this. And let me know what he says, okay?" "Will do."

Then, I steel myself, and I press the button on my phone that will hang up the call with Olivia and simultaneously answer Tristan's.

"Hello?" I say, trying to hide the way my voice shakes. *You can't show him weakness. You can't let him have that.*

"You're selling the house," Tristan bites out in lieu of a greeting, and I feel the color drain from my face at his frustrated tone that I'm all too familiar with.

"What?" I ask dumbly, completely knocked off balance by this entire situation.

"You're selling the house. Why?"

"Because I don't want to live there anymore?" It's a statement, but I say it like it's a question, like it should have been the logical conclusion for him to come to when he saw that the house was up for sale.

"But you got it in the divorce. Your *lawyer* fought so damn hard for that house. Why the *fuck* didn't you just let me keep it?" He raises the volume of his voice steadily as he says all of this, until he's nearly shouting. Belligerent. The way his words slur together at the end, I can tell that he's been drinking.

"I wasn't planning on selling it at first," I say truthfully. I can already feel myself shutting down, dissociating and disconnecting myself from this situation in some subconscious defense mechanism. It's better if I just don't feel any of it.

"What am I supposed to do now, Lydia? You got everything. We don't even have kids and you got everything."

"What is *that* supposed to mean?" My tone is probably a bit too forceful. I don't want to provoke him, but the fact that he's throwing the issue of kids in my face after months of not talking triggers something in me. I swallow, trying desperately to choke back tears of frustration.

"It means that you were the one who wanted the divorce anyways, and I don't know why you won. Clearly, I'm the one who's been wronged here." My detachment quickly gives way to pure, unfettered anger.

"Maybe you need some time for self-reflection then, Tristan. There's a reason why I filed for divorce, and that's what the courts saw. It's as simple as that. Now are we done here?"

"I can't believe you," He slurs, and I can hear music in the background. I wonder if it's just his TV, or if he's out somewhere. I don't know if it's worse if he's drinking alone or if he's out getting plastered with complete strangers. "How do you think that's okay without even telling me? That place was *ours*."

"Well, it's mine now. And I'm selling it. It's my house, so it's my decision." I try to sound confident in the hopes that it'll make me feel more confident.

"There are years of memories in that house. *Years.* You're telling me you're okay to just let those go?"

"Yes," I answer definitively, but in reality, the pain of the loss of it all is almost too much to bear.

"Our wedding night? The day we moved in? When we painted the kitchen?"

"Tristan, stop."

"What about that night the power went out? When we danced in the living room, when I lit those candles and we listened to music all night?"

"Please. I'm asking you to stop," My voice has taken on a pleading tone, and I hate myself for it. I hate myself for the way that I'm letting him get in my head. "Please."

"Why? You don't want to think about it?" He raises his voice again, all semblance of softness or regret lost. "Does it make you sad to think about everything we've lost?"

"You're drunk." I feel the tears hitting my cheeks before I realize that I'm crying.

"Of course I am! My wife left me, I don't have any reason not to be anymore!"

"Don't you *dare* put that on me," I notice the quiver in my voice, and that alone is enough to make me cry harder out of embarrassment. "You had a problem. You've had a problem this whole time."

"I don't have a problem. I would know if I had a problem."

"You go through a bottle of Vodka every few days."

"That's an exaggeration."

"I don't have time for this, Tristan! I'm selling the house. And I don't care about remembering those things because I don't *want to* remember those things," I say, trying to make my tone as sharp and biting as possible. But, in reality, I don't know that it's completely true. "So, leave me alone."

"You know what, *fuck* you, Lydia. I hope you're happy, okay? You fuckin' broke me. I waited for years for you to be ready to have kids. Waited for *years* for you to do whatever the fuck you were doing with your job. But you were always so absent. You would have been a terrible mother anyways. Have a nice life."

Beck hangs up. His words cut through me like a knife — I'm stunned into complete silence by the things he said. There was never a part of me that thought Tristan would be capable of saying things like that to me. He drank too much, was never home, we fought. But this? I want to try to convince myself that he's just saying it out of hurt, that he's just trying to get back at me in some twisted way.

And yet, his words still twist themselves around my mind, lodging there in an impenetrable seed of doubt. What if he's right? He found exactly the right button to press, exactly the right dagger to sharpen. He took my worst insecurities and put them on display, gutting me in the process. I don't know how to dig myself out of this. I'm shaking, the tears continuing to cascade down my face, and all I want is to not think. To act impulsively, to distract myself from my thoughts that continue to spiral out of my control.

So, in a moment of weakness, I decide to go find Beck.

Chapter 11

Lydia

"Hey, woah," Beck says as I approach him, looking up at me from where he's seated on the couch. I'm sure my eyes are bloodshot. It's obvious that I've been crying. But I can't bring myself to care. "You okay?"

"Fine. Never better, actually," I say, though I know my tone conveys otherwise. I sit down on the leather couch next to him, a scene of explorers in a cave playing on the TV in front of us. Probably I'm a bit too close for anything friendly, but my knee lands on his thigh, and his arm drapes across the couch behind me like we've done this a million times. It eases my nerves just a bit, being here with him. Maybe this wasn't such a bad idea after all. "What are you watching?"

"*The Mummy.*"

"Oh. I don't know if I've ever seen that."

"What?" Beck scoffs, "You've never seen *The Mummy?* I feel like I let you down when we were younger, I can't believe I didn't show you this one. It's a classic."

All I do is shrug, leaning a bit closer into his side. He doesn't seem to mind, or if he does, he doesn't show it. "You can make it up to me now," I reply simply.

"Beer?" Beck offers, raising a brow at me.

"Yes, please." At that, he leans down, procuring a Corona out of his father's very conveniently placed mini fridge. He pops the top, and I take a grateful swig, already feeling myself start to soften. "Thanks."

"Sure." I take a closer look at the TV once I'm settled. Immediately, I recognize the main actor in the movie.

"Oh! It's George!"

"Who?" Beck looks genuinely confused.

"George! Of the Jungle!" At this, he laughs, nearly choking on his beer.

"Oh, yeah. Brendan Fraser. That man is a national treasure."

"He *did* win an Oscar!"

"So, Ryan Gosling should be next," Beck muses, shooting me a look that lets me know that even though he might just be trying to impress me, he's not too proud to hide it.

"It's only right," I nod, "He deserves it."

"I still can't believe you haven't seen this." He settles back into the couch, then, his arm dropping from the back of the couch to wrap around my shoulders. I fight back a blush but allow myself to get at least somewhat comfortable.

"Isn't it scary though?" I question, "You know I don't like scary movies."

"It's not bad at all." As he says this, the scene changes — a scarab beetle has made its way under the skin of one of the archaeologists and is tunneling its way up, and I let out a screech, burying my face in Beck's shoulder. He laughs at me again, and I have to stop myself from punching his arm playfully. "Oh, wow, you weren't kidding, you really *can't* handle scary things."

"The bugs. Oh my God, that's horrible!"

"Aw. You're such a baby."

"Shut up."

"I'm just teasing," Beck remarks with a grin. "Come here, I'll protect you from the scary bugs." Then, his arms are around me, cradling me close to his chest. Almost on instinct, I wrap my arms around his torso and curl into his side. *What am I doing?* I don't know what to think, what to feel. My heart is racing now, and I take in a deep breath to try and center myself. But when I do, I get a whiff of his cologne; It's dark, woody, and musky with just the slightest hint of citrus. I want to drown myself in it, want to bury my face in his chest and breathe him in until I'm not sure where he begins and where I end. I remember all of the nights that we would spend in this very room, staying up too late and watching too many movies. Beck always insisted on something scary, and it always ended up just like this, with me clinging to him. Part of me wonders, now, if he was doing it on purpose the entire time.

"It's really like old times now," he says, nestling his head on top of mine. I laugh teasingly. Why do our minds have to always be on the same train of thought?

"It is, but I don't think that being scared is the part I wanted to relive."

"Oh, come on, this is fun. Do you remember the first time I showed you *Scream?*'

"I don't *want* to remember that," I shudder. That opening scene of Drew Barrymore still haunts me to this day.

"You were so scared that you cried," Beck erupts in a roar of laughter, throwing his head back like it's the funniest thing he's ever remembered. I scrunch my nose in false anger, and I'm not able to hold back this time — I punch his arm playfully and stick my tongue out at him. Beck feigns injury, rubbing his arm dejectedly. "Ow."

"That didn't hurt."

"It did, you're stronger than you look. I might need you to kiss it better." For some reason, I think I register his voice dropping a couple of octaves when he says this last part. Like he's trying to make it sound low and seductive. *Am I imagining this?*

"Really?" I ask, blinking rapidly. But when I see the teasing smirk plastered on his face, I know that he's getting exactly the reaction he wants out of me. I don't know what his goal is, or what kind of game he's trying to play, but I'm suddenly so *aware* of our proximity that I feel like I'm about to explode.

"Yeah, I think I just might." It's like he's magnetic, pulling me closer and closer to him, our faces only a foot or so apart. I swallow roughly, my eyes darting from his eyes to his lips and back to his eyes. The air feels thick and hot between us. I sit up a bit further, a dare and a question as I let myself inch closer and closer still, until my nose brushes against his, my eyelids heavy.

"I think I can manage that," I breathe. Then, we collide, our lips meeting in a kiss that's nothing if not fevered. I can hear my heartbeat in my ears. I'm far more sober than I was the first time that I kissed Beck Shepherd, but it's almost as if I want him even more than I did that first time. Like this has been an inevitability.

I brace myself against his chest, fisting at his shirt with my hands as I pull him closer. Beck's rough hands find the backs of my thighs as I sit up on my knees to straddle him, and I feel heat rushing through me at the sensation of his fingertips trailing up and up to the hem of my shorts between my thighs. His kisses become hard, unrelenting as he slides his tongue between my lips. Eagerly, I let mine move with his in a sort of dance, my need for him pooling in a heat that settles low between my thighs. I know that I'm wet even though he's barely touched me. Once Beck reaches the area where I need him the most, I have to hold back a whine. The layers of clothing between him and my slick center aren't going to do for very long, and as my hips rock against him, I know he gets the message.

Without warning, Beck lifts me up off his lap, laying me down on the couch. He only breaks our kiss for a moment, but when he kisses me again, it's hungry and full of desire, his hands trailing up and down my sides like he's trying to memorize me. One hand trails up and up my shirt, and I feel my breath hitch as he slides his hand underneath my bra, cupping my breast in his large hand. He squeezes and pinches the nipple, making me whimper softly, and then removes it to my dismay, bracing himself with it. In no more than a moment, though, his free hand is slipping past the waistband of my shorts.

"Beck, please," I whine, and I can tell that he knows exactly what I need by the glint in his eye. Slowly, so slowly, Beck's fingers move past the lace of my underwear to my slick center. He groans into my mouth as he runs his fingers between my folds, up and down, until they settle on my clit. He circles it slowly and so gently, the stimulation making me want him *just* that much more. I let my hips buck into his hand, trying so hard to make this last for myself, even though I could practically come undone already. My hands trail down his torso, finding the waistband of his shorts. I slip one past his boxers, finding his throbbing cock beneath the fabric. As I run my hand up and down his length, I notice his breath hitch, a delicate gasp leaving his parted lips.

"Holy *fuck*, Lydia." Once he finds his rhythm again, I wrap my hand around the base, and begin to pump him, our movements in tandem with one another. Little gasps and groans pass between our open mouths, and I feel myself start to be so consumed with my own need that I'm practically having to force myself to focus on stroking him. I want to make him feel good, want to keep making him keen and bite his lip, but then he adjusts his position, his other hand joining in his efforts to slide two fingers inside me. I'm completely gone, arching into him and moaning helplessly. I try to control my breathing as he fucks me with his fingers, but then he's kissing me again. It's so messy, so uncontrolled, and I feel my desire starting to crest, threatening to overtake me.

"Beck. Beck, please. I'm close, don't stop. Please, don't stop," I urge, my previous attempts at a handjob abandoned as I tangle my hands in his hair. He curls his fingers just the right way and then I'm coming around his fingers, my walls tightening and pulsing around him. I scream his name, but he silences me with another kiss, practically sucking on my tongue.

Beck rides me out through my high, but I still whine at the feeling of being empty again when he pulls his fingers out. I'm totally blissed out, fucked into oblivion, but I want to make him feel as good as he made me feel. So I press up onto my knees before he can make another move, pushing his chest until he's the one laying down. He looks up at me in surprise, but I grin down at him, making quick work of his belt.

"Your turn," I say, Beck's pupils dilating with pure desire as he looks up at me. Once I've got his shorts off,

I'm running one hand up and down his shaft, massaging his balls with the other.

And God, he is *big*. For a moment, I'm rethinking this. How the hell am I going to fit him in my mouth? He grabs my hair with one of his hands, though, holding it out of the way and tugging *just* the right amount to turn me on even further and encourage me more.

I lick a thick stripe up his length, relishing in the way he shudders and groans at just the smallest actions. Once I lick the tip, tasting all of the precum that's been so eagerly supplied for me, I take in a deep breath, steadying myself. I part my lips and start with just the tip, sucking gently and mewling around him. His grip on my hair tightens as I try to look like the picture of angelic innocence, taking more and more of him in as I try to work myself up to it. I let myself get most of his length slick before I wrap my hand around him again, spreading my saliva up and down his cock. Then, I'm taking in all of him that I can, hollowing out my cheeks and sucking eagerly as I pump the rest of him with my hand.

"Shit," Beck hisses, and I almost gag as he thrusts his hips up into my mouth involuntarily. I pick up the pace, then try to give him everything he wants, but the movements of his hips mean that his cock is practically hitting the back of my throat already. My eyes start to water, but the additional wetness from my spit makes it somewhat easier to thrust my mouth down his length. I suck hard, threatening to choke with each thrust of his hips that sends him deeper and deeper into my throat.

Tears sting my eyes as I suck harder and harder, but with another shuddering groan, he lifts my head up by the hair, a *pop* sounding as his length falls from my mouth.

"I don't want to come until I've fucked you, Lydia. Come here," He rasps, voice somewhere between demanding and needy. Without another word, I shimmy out of my shorts and underwear, kicking them to the floor. I want him more than I've ever wanted anyone else in my life, and as I'm climbing up to line my hips up with his, he's leaning over to pick his shorts up off the ground. For a moment, I pause, confusion evident on my face. But he's quick to show me what he's reaching for, fishing a condom out of his wallet.

"What? You think you're the only one who's allowed to be prepared on this trip?" At that, I can't help but laugh, pressing my lips to his again with a needy kiss.

"Very funny," I tease as he opens the condom and rolls it down his length, hands finding their way to my hips once he's done. Finally, I line myself up with him, humming so softly as I take my time to adjust to the size again. Luckily, I'm already wet and perfectly loose, and his length slides into me far easier than the first time. He fills me up so nicely, and I whimper, letting myself just *sit* for a moment in this want and contentment as I lean over to press a chaste kiss to his lips. Beck's hand finds the back of my neck, holding me there as he deepens the kiss, while I start to grind my hips up and down his length ever so slowly. I clench around him, and he gasps into the kiss, our lips barely brushing as I ride him. I know without a doubt that I'm going to come for a second time that night when his hands move to grab my ass, helping me along in my movements as I whimper softly, picking up the pace.

Then, Beck bucks his hips up beneath me, driving himself in even further. He hits a sensitive spot in my core, and I cry out.

"Beck!" I cry, letting myself lean over even further, hands finding their way into his curls. I'm essentially hopeless, and he must know, because he takes the lead easily, thrusting up into me and picking up the pace. We meet each other thrust for thrust, my lips sliding past his as I beg into his open mouth, pleading for him to make me come a second time that night.

"I'm so close, Beck, I'm—" I gasp, my words muffled as I bury my face in his chest to stifle my loud whines. Then, he takes over fully, thrusting up into me relentlessly with an almost animalistic ferocity. The way he's moaning, his breathing heavy and his gasps getting louder and louder, I know he's close too. Beck hits that spot in my core again, and I cry out helplessly, my walls pulsing and clenching around him as I reach my second high of the night. He moans out my name in bliss as he fucks me through his own high, little beads of sweat collecting on his forehead as he works me through to the very end.

When he finally stills, I let myself collapse against him fully, my heart thudding ceaselessly with the exertion. Once he catches his breath, he lets his hands trail up the back of my shirt so slowly, touching me like I'm something delicate and fragile.

"Beck..." I can barely get his name out.

"Yes?" He says gently, brushing a strand of hair out of my face.

"I can't feel my legs."

At that, Beck laughs uproariously, pressing a gentle kiss to my lips. He doesn't hesitate, though, sliding out of me to pull me down onto the couch next to him. Once he takes off the condom and discards it, he pulls me against his chest, arms wrapping around me from behind.

"Better?" He asks, voice still hoarse as I let myself play with his fingers, sighing contentedly.

"Much better."

So, he holds me, just like that, pressing gentle kisses against the back of my neck.

I don't think about Tristan the entire time. About the terrible things he said to me, about how he could be drunk and off sleeping with some random girl he met at a bar right now. I'm glad that my plan to forget worked.

But, as I settle into Beck's arms, completely content and wanting nothing but *more*, I can't help but ask myself if it might have worked a little too well.

Chapter 12

Beck

We decided to get dressed again pretty quickly after letting ourselves breathe. I don't know how to process it all, that we just did that in a far more conscious state of mind and that I'm still here, laying on the couch with Lydia and holding her. I find myself so lost in my mind that I haven't even paid any attention to the rest of the movie, the sun starting to sink below the horizon out the window. What I *do* notice, though, is Lydia. She's usually glad to talk, even when we're just sitting around, and I'm suddenly afraid that I've done something wrong. I run my fingers through her hair delicately, looking down at her inquisitively as I do so.

"You're being quiet," I say finally, pressing a gentle kiss to the top of her head.

"Am I?"

"You are."

"Well, what did you want to talk about, then?" Lydia turns onto her back, then, and for a moment I'm disappointed not to be holding her anymore. But she smiles up at me, and drapes my arm across her torso, which quiets my mind. I'm still curious, though, as to what had her so upset before this.

"You seemed... you seemed very tense earlier."

"Oh."

"Any particular reason why that is?" I ask gently. A beat passes, and Lydia looks like she's weighing her options, fighting some battle in her mind. After a moment, she sighs, looking up at me somewhat dejectedly.

"Tristan called me."

"I see."

She goes quiet again and averts her gaze. Is that all this was to her, then? A hookup to forget the fact that she just went through a divorce?

No, I tell myself, don't *think like that. All it will do is make you miserable.*

"Do I need to drive back home and kick his ass?" I ask, finally breaking the silence.

"What did he do?"

"No, he was... he was drunk. He did say some pretty terrible things, though."

"What did he say to you?" Lydia's eyes finally meet mine again, and I immediately regret asking once I see the tears starting to well up and the wry smile on her face.

"That I was too absent and would be a terrible mother."

The words feel like a gut punch. How could someone who'd claimed to love her at some point say something so *cruel?* So obviously untrue? I prop myself up on my elbow, jaw clenched as I shake my head.

"The option to beat him up is looking better and better by the second."

"Yeah, well. It doesn't necessarily make any of what he said untrue either way," Lydia mumbles, and I feel my heart shattering. Surely, she can't actually believe that. "I mean, he's probably right. I would be a terrible mother. I don't even know if I have a single motherly bone in my body." She lets out a humorless laugh, and wipes at her eyes where tears have started to fall. Without hesitation, I wrap my arms around her again, pulling her flush against my chest.

"Hey, no. Don't cry. Please don't cry."

"I *hate* crying," She sniffles, "Jesus. This is why I never do this."

"I'm sorry. I shouldn't have asked."

"No, it's okay," She reassures me, pulling back from my chest to wipe her eyes. "It's not your fault. He's the one that said it."

"He's wrong, by the way," I say decisively. Lydia blinks a couple of times at this, clearly confused.

"You think so?"

"I *know* so. You would be an excellent mother. Lydia, you care so much. You've got the biggest heart out of anyone I know." I pause for a moment as I try to find the words, my eyes searching hers. Then, I remember the perfect example. "There was a time back when we were kids that we all wanted to go out and catch fireflies. Me, you, Amber, Liv — we all ran outside right as the sky was darkening and you were so excited. Probably the most excited out of all of us. You called them the 'pretty bugs', but as soon as we started catching them and having our parents put them in jars, you started to cry. I remember you saying something—"

"Just because they're pretty bugs, it doesn't mean we get to do whatever we want with them." My smile is wide, and I let out a small chuckle.

"Really, you were wise beyond your years. How did you come up with that? We were only, what? Seven or eight years old at the time?"

"I can't remember. I just remember that because my dad always used to say it after the fact. Well, he'd call things that were a little bit too fancy for us to be around the 'pretty bugs'. We'd go to the Smithsonian and when I would want to touch everything, he would tell me no, and then ask me why he'd said no. The answer was always 'they're pretty bugs'."

"That's so sweet."

"Dad did have his moments."

Lydia falls silent again, and I rake my fingers aimlessly through her hair. On some level, I think I already knew this, but when it comes to the forefront of my mind, I'm taken aback by it all the same — *I would do anything to make her happy.*

"Well, what are we going to do about this?" I finally say, "We can't have you being miserable on our first night of vacation."

"Beck, I'm fine. Don't worry about it, seriously."

"I'm going to worry about it, though. I'm determined to show you a good time, Dee, because you damn well deserve it." I earn a small smile from her at this, and my heart soars.

"Okay, so what's your plan, Shepherd?"

"Dancing, if you're up for it. A movie if you're not."

I can see the gears turning in Lydia's head as she weighs the options. It's not too late for us to go some-where fun, since it's barely 9:00, but I'm secretly hoping that she'll want to stay in. I resolve to do whatever is going to make her happy, though, and am content with that decision. Whatever she chooses is going to be good enough for me, I decide, and when she snuggles closer to me, I feel like my heart is about to leap out of my chest.

"Well. Isn't there a second *Mummy* movie that we can watch?"

***

I wake up next to Lydia for the second time and I'm almost halfway convinced that I'm still dreaming. But then her eyes flutter open into mine and there isn't anything that I can do but smile at her. The soft morning light shines through the window and onto where her hair is fanned out on the pillow next to mine, and I have to resist myself from running my hands through it. She smiles over at me, then, and I think for a moment that I don't think I've ever seen someone so beautiful.

Before we finished *The Mummy Returns*, Lydia fell asleep on the couch. I'd carried her up to her bed, but she mumbled something once we got there about wanting to stay with me instead. About not wanting to sleep alone. So, I obliged, and once we were in such close quarters again, we ended up having sex for the second time that night. I'm not about to complain about that, though, especially not when she's stretching out next to me so lazily and contentedly.

"Good morning," I say, grinning over at Lydia.

"Oh, it's you."

I chuckle at that, pressing a gentle kiss to her forehead. "Were you expecting it to be someone else?"

"Of course not. I was just dreaming about this really hunky blonde man being in the bed, actually, but it seems like it really is just you after all."

"Ouch."

"Teasing. You're a hunky blonde, too, Beck."

"Wow, I feel so much better now," I deadpan, voice monotone.

"Good. Wouldn't want to bruise your ego there, big guy," Lydia says with a teasing smile, patting my chest lightly.

"You're a pest."

"And you're insufferable." I playfully rustle her hair, before I stand up and stretch a bit myself.

"Do you want breakfast? I'm starving."

"We didn't go to the grocery store."

"We don't have to. There are coffee shops here now, you know." For a long time, the only locations on the cape were mom-and-pop stores and the occasional raw bar. But, in order to appeal to a younger generation of vacationers, trendy brunch restaurants and coffee shops have started to pop up over the past few years. "I'll have to take you to go see them."

"You sure know the way to a girl's heart. Cute and overpriced coffee." I can't help that this makes me feel giddy, almost like a teenager with a crush. I guess that deep down, I really am still just that high school kid who's in love with his best friend. But I'm trying hard not to get my hopes up, so I chastise myself for even thinking about it, resigning myself to just let myself go for once in my life.

The coffee shop we go to isn't that far from my parents' house. They'd recommended it to me as one they'd started to visit on their last trip down, and I see why. It's the perfect combination of beach theming and a standard coffee shop design, with couches and small circular tables for patrons. The Beach Boys play over the speakers, and vintage surf posters adorn the walls. Plus, the menu is written on half of a surfboard.

Lydia: "God almighty. For these prices, this *better* be the best coffee I've ever had." She's right — a latte is almost seven dollars, which seems a little bit ridiculous, even for "ethically sourced coffee beans".

"They don't have any competition," I say, scanning the menu to see that all of the drink names are similarly beach themed. "This is essentially a coffee shop monopoly, I think."

"Do you think this coffee shop is the Cape San Blas equivalent of the Boardwalk or Park Place cards in Monopoly, then?"

"We can only hope."

Once we arrive at the counter, I order the Riptide (americano) and Lydia opts for a Surfin' Safari (caramel latte). We also get a couple of ham and cheese croissants for breakfast and sit down at a table while we wait for our food and our drinks to be brought out. Lydia and I are in the middle of a discussion of the merits of whether or not records should be hung on walls

(we both agreed that they should be stored properly, even if they weren't being listened to), when the barista who took our order walks up to us. In passing, she makes a comment about how cute we are together — and much to my dismay, I see the panic appear across Lydia's face.

"Oh — uh, thank you," she says gently, a tight smile on her face.

"We're very lucky." At that, the barista nods knowingly and walks away. And Lydia shoots me a look that does not hide the way she feels in the slightest.

"*God*, that's awkward," Lydia says, visibly cringing before taking a sip of her coffee. I feel my heart sink. "I mean, what are you even supposed to say in situations like that? 'Oh, no, we're actually just friends, but it's recently become very complicated as we have started sleeping together. But don't worry, we've decided that it doesn't mean anything and that we will be keeping it casual.'"

She laughs, then, waving it all off. I try to look casual, try to laugh with her, but I can't ignore the fact that I'm wondering why it seems to be so *comical* to her that people would assume we were dating. Is the idea really that foreign to her?

"Yeah," I nod, "People really shouldn't make assumptions."

And just like that, I realize it; I'm all the way ahead of myself here with no way to stop it.

Lydia clearly doesn't feel the same things I do, and I'm making something out of nothing.

Catapulting us straight towards disaster.

Chapter 13

Lydia

Once we're done with coffee, Beck decides he wants to spend the rest of the day fishing. I don't have to hide my distaste for spending my time on this activity, because Beck spared me the trouble by telling me that I didn't have to come with him. That I should go to some of the shops in town and look around before we head to the beach tomorrow. So, I spend the first half of my day shopping, looking through stores for little trinkets that I could bring back to my family members as souvenirs or for interesting pieces of local artwork that I could decorate the house with.

The house. The house that I no longer own. The house that I just took great pains to get everything out of that hasn't even generated very much attention yet on the market. And just like that, shopping seems like more of a chore than an actually enjoyable activity.

While I'm walking, though, I realize with only a small amount of horror that I probably (no, *definitely*) need a wax before I let Beck see me in a bikini. The fact that he's already seen, well, *everything* makes no difference to me. If it's visible outside of the swimsuit, it's got to go. Since Beck was staying at the house to fish, he'd let me take his family's Jeep, so I hop in and make my way to the nearest wax studio.

The lobby is nice enough, with all of the miniature water features and copies of *InStyle* that can't be any less than ten years old piled high on the coffee table in the waiting room. The lamplight illuminates the space in a way that somehow says *'You're welcome here! It's homey!'* and *'This might be an actual torture dungeon.'* at the same time. The receptionist is kind, though, and when my name is called, I head down the hallway to Room 4, with its sparkling sign and friendly exterior.

I always forget how much getting waxed hurts until I'm actually doing it. I've never given birth before, but I've heard people say that during the process, your brain blocks out all of the memories of the pain and replaces them with happy ones so that you'll want to do it again. I kind of wonder if it's the same situation here, but just at a much lesser scale.

I also forget how uncomfortable it is to be spread eagle on a table in front of a complete stranger until I'm actually there doing it. My waxer, Jenna, introduces herself as she walks in, completely unphased by the fact that all of my goods are on display.

"We're just doing the bikini line today, right?"

"Yep," I say, with a bit of a *pop* to the p for emphasis.

"Okay, great — have you shaved since the last time you've been waxed?" I hate this question. They ask it every single time, and it makes me feel weird, mostly because I don't understand the difference that it makes. That, and I know that it's these people's *jobs* to do this, but I also don't love to talk about my personal grooming habits so openly.

"Not completely," I start, "I usually just trim. It's more of a control thing for me, honestly." Mentally, I chide myself for this statement. What does it even *mean*? Those are the kinds of things that I wish I could keep to myself sometimes, but they mostly just come blurting out anyway with no real reason.

"Oh," Jenna raises a brow as she crosses the room to turn on the wax pot. "Do we need to unpack that?"

"What, you're asking me to vent to you?" I say with an uncomfortable laugh. "Offering me a free therapy session?"

Jenna must pick up on my unease, because she waves a casual hand, turning back to what she's doing at the table. "Honey, that's practically the second line in my job description. You wouldn't believe some of the things that these people tell me while I'm staring right at their privates."

"Huh."

"I'm serious! Ask any of the girls here, they'll tell you the same thing. Something about how if you're already bearing it all to a complete stranger, that you might as well just tell them your deepest and darkest secrets." When I think about it that way, it actually makes total sense. There's no room for shyness when you're already fully exposed. I'm airing out my vagina already. Might as well air out my secrets, too.

"That's a fair point. I mean, you're not going to remember me or any of this tomorrow."

"Exactly. So. Why is it you think you feel the need to always be in control?"

So, I tell her everything. I'm more open with Jenna than I am with my actual therapist who I pay upwards of two hundred dollars to see every month. And she's right, it's honestly kind of freeing — she just stands there, stirring the wax in the warmer and listening to me tell her all of the details about my divorce, reacting to me viscerally with gasps and shakes of her head as if she's listening to a soap opera unfolding in real time.

In a sense, I guess, its kind of has been that way. Messy hookups, divorce, family drama, people getting married and having babies. The only thing that's missing would be me doing something like shooting Tristan and him miraculously coming back to life two or three seasons later.

Or me throwing a drink in his face. But I digress.

"Wow." Jenna whistles once I finish speaking, dipping a popsicle stick into the wax and smearing it over the top of my pubic bone. At first, I wince at the heat, but then I settle into it. I kind of equate it to sticking my finger into one of those scented wax warmers that my mom used to have when I was a kid, but I don't say anything about that, of course. "That's a lot."

"You could say that again."

"So why did you decide to go into law, then? If you don't like arguing?" I didn't even realize that I'd somehow gotten into complaining about my career during my earlier rant, so her question catches me off guard momentarily.

"Well," I start, "I've always loved to learn. And with law, I'm always learning something new. I'm always studying, always having to research. So, I guess until recently, doing that and climbing the ladder at work was enough for me. I just..." I think about Olivia and her engagement. About Amber and Melanie and their adoption. It's all been staring me in the face, the reasons for every single one of my impulsive actions recently, and I've been too afraid to name it. Too afraid to face it, to give it power. "Everyone's lives are moving on without me, and I feel like I've just taken so many steps backward. Even with the promotion. So, I'm reevaluating.

It just doesn't... it doesn't feel the way it— *Ouch*."

"Sorry!" Jenna chirps, which *completely* does not make up for the fact that she just ripped hair out of my body with no precursor whatsoever, but I give her a tight smile and a nod anyways. "Should have warned you. So, you've got feelings for your best friend, you're dissatisfied at work, and you recently realized that your job and your promotion had become an excuse for you to distract yourself from your disappointing marriage rather than your actual passion. Is that right?"

"That pretty much sums it up," I say, void of any expression or emotion. It sounds so bleak hearing it come from someone else that it almost threatens to make me spiral. My distress must be showing on my face, though, because Jenna quickly applies more wax, before changing the topic.

"So, what *do* you enjoy, though?" She asks me, and she sounds genuinely curious about it.

"You like learning, what else?"

"I love to travel." I don't miss a beat when I tell her this. Travel is always my answer when someone asks me what my passion in life is, what it is that makes me feel truly alive. "I've always loved traveling, actually."

"What about traveling?"

"Well, everything, really. Seeing new places. Doing new things. Making memories and documenting them. I also really love to give people souvenirs, actually," I smile briefly, "Like, my sister, for instance. She's obsessed with coffee, so I always get her something coffee-related anywhere I go."

"You know," Jenna muses, "There are ways that you can make *traveling* your career." At this, I can't help but laugh dryly. "What? I'm serious! There are travel bloggers, travel photographers, travel *vloggers*. People love that stuff! You could even write for a travel magazine."

"Right. I'm not the creative one, that's my sister. She's the one that does all of the writing and things."

"What does she do?"

"She runs a short story publication."

"Well, there you go!" She says it like it's an epiphany, like she's a scientist making a discovery in a lab rather than a woman who until previously I had not met who is now eye-level with my vagina. "Couldn't she hire you as a travel researcher? Or even a travel writer? You've got the inside connection, girl. You're telling me you've *really* never thought about that?"

And I *have* thought about it. But, at the same time, the thought of asking my older sister for a job makes my skin crawl. Or for help of *any* kind, as a matter of fact. Not because she won't give it to me, I know she will, but I know how she sees me. It's the same way everyone sees me. She sees me as successful, as a self-starter, as one of those girls who proves that women really *can* be in a male-dominated field and be successful. Not only Olivia, but my entire family sees me that way. I'm sure of it. So, to me, it's a non-starter.

But *God*, if it isn't tempting sometimes.

"That... that kind of thing has occurred to me, yes," I say after a moment, giving her a bit of a wry smile. I can tell that she can read me, the whole *I-really-would-rather-die* of it all probably deeply evident on my features.

"Well, don't waste your life being miserable. That's what I say. Oh, I'm about to pull this strip by the way," Even with the heads up, I still wince, but I try not to let it be as obvious as it was the first time. "You don't need to measure yourself based on the successes of other people around you. You also don't need to feel like you're only stuck doing something because you're 'supposed' to be doing that thing. We all reinvent ourselves every day, honey. No one's path is linear."

I definitely didn't expect such profound advice from this 40-something waxer who I'd never met before. For a moment, I didn't know what to say. Surely, if Jenna is happy where she's at, then I can find things that will make me happy too.

"Thank you," I hope that I sound as genuine as I want to. "That... that's actually really helpful."

"What did I tell you? Second line of my job description. Okay, pulling this strip."

***

After Beck and I reconvene at the house for dinner, we decide to head down to a nearby ice cream shop and take a walk-through town. There isn't a cloud in the sky, and the sun lingers only slightly above the horizon, reflecting orange and yellow against the ocean.

My family have always been what I like to refer to as 'beach sunset people'. Which is a particular subset of beachgoers who *specifically* schedule the latter half of their day around getting back to the shore to watch the sun sink below the water. And while the sight is beautiful, I've never really understood the appeal. I'm generally happy if I see it once on a trip, because as much as I do enjoy the sunset, I've always found that level of dedication a little... over the top.

But tonight, it kind of makes sense to me. Tonight, the sky dances with reds and pinks and oranges in a watercolor display. Our view is perfect from the bench we've selected, and I'm fully content at this moment. We eat our ice cream in silence, for a while, children and families still buzzing around us as they go about their nightly routines of shopping and eating dinner and all of the usual beach activities.

For the first time in a long time, I feel unhurried. I will this moment to last forever, just us, here and now, in one of my favorite places in the entire world. I look over to Beck and catch his eye. He smiles at me, then, in a way that lets me know that he's feeling exactly the same way. He drapes his free arm lazily across the back of the bench, wordlessly offering me a taste of his ice cream (he got Rocky Road, and I got mint chocolate chip). I accept and nod gratefully, humming contentedly as I settle into his side a bit more, propping my feet up on the bench.

"So," I start, finally breaking the silence, "Beach Day tomorrow, right? How's the weather going to be?"

"Last I checked, it looked like it would be clear all day, but this is Florida. If you remember, the weather here is pretty much unpredictable." He fiddles with the sleeve of my shirt absentmindedly as he talks, and I have to suppress a giggle.

"Yeah, that's a good point."

"Where did you go off to this morning?" He asks, and I freeze for a moment. The thought of telling him that I got waxed seems strange to admit to him, for some reason, even though we'd been naked together twice now.

"Oh. Uh, nowhere important," I shrug, trying my best to sound and look nonchalant. "Just went out to get a manicure—" When I gesture towards him, I see that the plain polish that's on my nails is chipped and clearly old. *God, I really need to stop biting my nails and leave my cuticles alone.* Quickly, I pivot. "Pedicure, I mean. I went to get a pedicure. I don't know *why* I said manicure." Thank *God* for close-toed heels.

"Okay," He quirks an eyebrow and laughs, definitely taking note of my strange behavior.

"I could have come with you. Heather used to drag me out to get pedicures with her all the time.

It was kind of fun, actually."

"Right." Everything keeps coming back to Heather. I can't be jealous of Beck's dead wife. That would be morbid and horrific. So, I shove the thought down, but am still unable to suppress that gnawing feeling in the pit of my stomach. I feel like I'm taking advantage of him.

Using him to 'have fun' on this vacation without having any real concern for *his* feelings. Clearly, this place... it was *special* to him and to Heather. They have memories here. Firsts in their marriage that will never leave him. And yet here I am, the sad divorced girl, making him take pity on *me* .

Beck must notice my extended silence, because he nudges my side, a playful expression on his face when he speaks again. "They felt pretty good, actually. The pedicures. But I've got really ticklish feet. One time, I accidentally splashed my foot water at the lady doing it because she was tickling me so much."

"Beck, I know we've slept together and all, but please do not talk to me about your feet." I visibly cringe but laugh anyway. "And for the love of God, never ever say the words 'foot water' again."

"Hey, you started it." "I hate you."

"Didn't seem to hate me last night—" At this, I deliver a playful punch to his arm. "*Ow* .

You're stronger than you look, you know. That actually kind of hurts when you do that."

"Right, because all 6 '4 and two hundred and fifty pounds of pure muscle of you are definitely affected by my scrawny little noodle arms."

"Selling yourself short. You could be one of those female MMA fighters."

"Wow, every little girl's dream." My laughter is practically constant by this point. I had forgotten how easy it was with him, how practiced he was in saying exactly the right things that would always get me rolling. I've even forgotten what I was upset about up until then. "Hey, I've got a question, though."

"What's up?"

"I've been thinking about what you said. About wanting to go out. Dancing." Beck visibly perks up when I suggest it, like the idea of getting all dressed up to take me out is the thing he's been waiting for this whole time.

"Yeah?"

"Well, I would be up for it tonight. If you are, that is." Beck grins and nods, pulling me into his side and pressing a kiss to my temple.

"I think that sounds like a blast."

There's only one club in town. Truly, though, calling it a 'club' is generous — it's just one of those beach bars that has live music and an outdoor bar for dancing. But we dance anyway, and it's more crowded than I expected it to be. String lights stretch out from the stage across the crowd and paper lanterns hang from the trees, illuminating the night in a way that's nothing short of dreamy.

I probably should have expected Beck to be a good dancer, but for some reason, when he's spinning me around to the rendition of [insert song by artist] that they're playing, I'm swept off my feet all the same. His hands guide me effortlessly when I would have been clumsy otherwise. I'm far too aware of every one of his movements; Up and down my sides, rubbing my hips, spinning me around to press against him fully. His arms wrap tight around my waist as we sway, and he leaves a trail of kisses down my neck to my shoulder that have me melting under his touch. It's like he's an expert with me, like he knows exactly the ways to move me to make me want him. Before I know it, I'm leaning back against his chest, whispering in his ear that I want him to take me home.

So, he does. We have sex two more times that night, tender and wanting and full of desire. Beck is almost insatiable when it comes to me, I realize. If I hadn't been completely spent, if I had said one word to him about wanting to go again, he would have done so gladly.

When I fall asleep, I am cradled in his arms, completely and perfectly content.

Chapter 14

Beck

We finally made it out to the beach on the third day of our trip. I liked that our styles of travel are rather similar, particularly when it came to beach vacations — neither Lydia nor I find it necessary to spend all day sitting out in the sun, especially not every single day. Plus, in DC, we're only about an hour away from public beach access at Sandy Point, so we're more concerned about maximizing our time seeing the sights rather than getting sunburnt.

Or, at least, I thought that I liked the fact that Lydia also didn't care to spend all day baking in the sun. Until I see her in a bikini, that is.

I'm busy setting up our umbrella, so I don't notice at first when she's taking off her cover-up and putting on sunscreen. But once I do, I realize that I'm basically no better than a teenage boy when it comes to her; I remember when I used to sneak glances at her when we were in high school on these vacations, her slender legs and toned stomach from her time spent on the swim team used to give me plenty of... well, *inspiration* for when my mind would inevitably wander. Now, though, she's curvy, soft around the edges, and though I don't *have* to imagine what's underneath anymore, I find myself doing so all the same.

But, apparently, I'm not as careful as I used to be.

"Beck, can you get my shoulders? I can't — oh. See something you like, Shepherd? My eyes are up here." Lydia laughs, and I feel my face color.

"Dee, I'm just a man. I can't help it." I grin slyly over at her, trying my best to play it cool even in spite of my glaringly obvious attraction to her. Even still, I stand up, taking the bottle of sunscreen from her.

"Turn around," I instruct, and she obliges. I try not to think too much about how badly I want to kiss all the way down the back of her neck as I spread the sunscreen across her shoulders and down her back, rubbing the lotion into her skin gently. But it's so hard not to picture all of the things that I want to do to her, particularly now that I know exactly the way she sounds when I do those things.

"I think you got it," she says with a giggle after a moment, and I clear my throat, snapping back to myself. It has always been far too easy for me to get lost in daydreams, particularly when they are about her. "Thanks."

"Yeah, of course. We can't have you getting burnt."

"Yeah, then you'd have to rub aloe on me later, too. How unfortunate." I shoot her a daring glance and see that she's wiggling her eyebrows at me playfully as she settles down into her beach chair, a book in one hand and a beer in the other. I laugh at her expression, shaking my head.

"Tease."

"Takes one to know one."

"Right, okay." Then, I pull my shirt off over my head, tossing it into the beach bag in one fluid motion. I catch Lydia's eyes on me this time, looking at me like I'm a meal.

"Oh, two can play this game. Eyes are up here, sweetheart."

"What?" She says once she looks up from my chest to my face, blinking rapidly. She looks like a deer in the headlights, and I laugh again, shaking my head.

"Oh, this is going to be fun."

The beach isn't too crowded for the time of day. At least, it's not as crowded as I had expected it to be, since the cape is a popular vacation spot for families who are on their summer breaks. It's 10:00 by the time we're fully finished setting up, and the closest people to us are a good twenty feet away, which is a solid distance of privacy when it comes to Florida beaches.

Fluffy white clouds traverse their way across the sky, unhurried, but still with a sense of purpose and direction to their otherwise meandering nature. A popsicle melts down a boy's arm that's sitting adjacent to us with his family, bright red streaks of sticky sugar coating his hand. I remember the simplicity of that time in my life, when all I had to worry about was which popsicle, I would have next. That's the thing that being here always does for me. It transports me back in time.

The day passes slowly. We read, we eat the sandwiches we packed for lunch, we take occasional trips down to the water to cool off from the relentless nature of the Florida sun. Lydia is almost definitely outpacing me in the amount of beer she's drinking, but I don't make any comments about this. After all, she's always been able to hold her booze better than me, and still is. My two Coronas have me somewhat buzzed, but she seems completely unphased as she sips on her fourth.

"Beck, did you know there's a pottery studio not too far from here? Like, thirty minutes away or so," Lydia asks as she's scrolling on her phone, and I know that I must have visibly perked up when she said it, because she smiles over at me.

"Is there?" I lean over to see the screen as she turns her phone to me. "Huh, it must be new."

"Well, would you have necessarily been looking to go to a pottery studio last time you were here?"

"That... yeah, that's a good point. Not really."

"What do you say we go, then?" I can tell that she's excited by the prospect of it, and even though I only *somewhat* cringe internally at the thought of going somewhere other than my favorite studio in town, I know that I'll go if it will make her happy. "I'd love to see you in your element."

"Oh, you would?"

"I very much would. And you could teach me. It would be hot, like that scene in *Ghost* with Patrick Swayze."

"That's pretty much the entire reason I started doing pottery, anyway," I say, pretending to be thoughtful as I take a swig of my beer. "To recreate that scene. I just had to find a willing participant."

"Wait, was it really?" I throw my head back and laugh.

"No, I'm messing with you. Why are you so gullible?"

"Shut up."

"Make me."

"In your dreams, Shepherd."

"It doesn't seem too far-fetched from reality—" At this, she hits me in the chest with the back of her hand lightly. "*Ouch.*"

"Well, I think it'll be hot anyways," She shrugs, and then gasps, as if she's just come to a shocking realization. "We can even play *Take My Breath Away* in the background!"

"That's *Top Gun*, not *Ghost*." As I say this, I notice a seagull stealing a piece of bread from a sandwich someone had left unattended. Amateurs.

"Oh. Why did I think it was *Ghost?*"

"I have no idea, but I'm pretty sure that's just you.

"Dang."

***

The next day, we make the trip over to the neighboring town to visit the studio after breakfast. The place that Lydia found, aptly called "Sky & Ocean", is exactly as I pictured it would be. Light blue walls and cream-colored paintings line the rows of brick red clay wheels on stone-colored tables. Despite the differences from the vivid decorations of my home studio, I still feel welcome here, and still find myself ready to create. Natural light streams through large windows, making the space feel even more airy and welcoming. The only other people in the studio are the owners, who check us in and show us to the wheels where we'll be throwing, and a few older ladies who I can only assume are locals.

The earthy smell of clay grounds me. I don my apron and sit on my stool, dipping my hands in the bowl of water that's centered between us. Effortlessly, I center my clay, deciding that I will finalize whether it is that I'm making a bowl or a vase or a pitcher as I go. I'll let the clay do the talking — I'll just listen to what it has to say.

"Okay," Lydia says to me after a moment, poking at the clay with one finger inquisitively. "So, what do I do here?" I turn my attention away from my piece to her, letting the wheel continue on, the formless lump spinning on top of it.

"You're going to want to wet your hands first," I tell her, gesturing to the bowl in front of us.

"Alright." She dips one hand, then the other. She regards her dripping hands with some distaste as she holds them out awkwardly in front of her. I have to stifle a laugh. "I don't know what to do with my hands."

"You pick up the clay with them."

"Oh."

"Now step on the wheel." Lydia follows my instructions, and her eyes widen, the movement seeming to take her by surprise.

"Okay, it's spinning."

"Yeah, it is. Now, you just have to kind of... throw the clay down in the center."

"What happens if I *miss* the center?" She seems truly panicked by this, like her entire day depends on whether or not she gets the clay in the right position on the wheel.

"You won't. But the reason that it's in the center is so that it doesn't go flying off the side of the wheel or take on some kind of weird shape."

"What if it turns into a weird shape even though I center it right?"

"Well, then you'll just have a very unique looking bowl. Now throw." Lydia obliges then, the clay hitting the surface of the wheel with a wet *thunk* . It's only somewhat off center, but she beams up at me, her pride evident on her face, and I beam.

"Good," I say, nodding approvingly as I motion to my own wheel, showing her my hand placement for her to replicate. "Now you can start to shape the clay."

"Is this the part where you put your hands over mine and stand behind me and breathe down my neck and stuff?"

"You were really serious about this *Ghost* thing, weren't you?"

"*Maybe* I fantasized about it a little when I first saw the movie."

"I knew you were only using me for my body and for my skill with clay."

"Just shut up and come over here."

I roll my eyes playfully but leave my clay sitting on the wheel as I move behind her, leaning down and positioning my hands on top of hers.

"Pressure here," I mutter into her ear, stroking the pad of my thumbs over the back of hers, right on the knuckle, feeling her lean back against me. "With your thumbs. Your goal is to make a little divot on the top so that you can start to shape it and make it taller and wider."

"Like this?" She pushes her thumbs down, then, and I let her take the lead, lightening up on the gentle input I'd been providing with mine.

"Good. Yes. Now spread your hands apart. Let it take shape."

My eyes stay fixed on Lydia's hands as she starts to work the clay, almost a natural as I watch it take form. But then she's pressing back into me just a little bit further, letting her body weight sink into mine, and I hum softly at the proximity of it. The closeness. Almost involuntarily, I let my fingertips start to trail up and up the length of her bare arms, a ghost of a touch as I feel myself falling into it, into the sensation of just being *near* her. She's a siren and I'm a sailor drawn helplessly to her call.

I let my head dip ever so slightly, lips carefully brushing against the notch where her neck and her shoulder meet. I feel her tremble beneath me, clearly just as affected by this as I am, and hear her gasp when I breathe her name against her skin. It's only a whisper, just a hint of the word, but the implication behind it is pure and unfettered *want.*

Before I know it, my hand has trailed its way all the way up her arm, until I'm cupping her face and turning her just that little bit more towards me. We kiss, sweet and hot and urgent, her lips slotting perfectly against mine. I'm so lost in it that I'm almost unaware that we're in public until I hear the sound of someone clearing their throat beside us. I pull away quickly, meeting eyes with the elderly man two tables down from us. I know that my face is red, and so is Lydia's. We giggle like teenagers who got caught holding hands behind the bleachers.

"Ah, uh, sorry about that," I say, giving him an apologetic smile. My laughter does nothing but crescendo, though, when I see the mess that I've made — I've left a trail of gray smudges up the length of both of Lydia's arms and a handprint on the side of her face.

"What? What is it?"

"Nothing, I just accidentally turned you into a contestant on *Survivor* who ends up covered in mud."

"Either that, or I'm just your canvas," she says, tilting her head up at me. Her voice is low and thick, and I'm immediately picturing with nothing but paint on her body to show every single place that I'd touched her. In our distraction, Lydia's formless lump of clay had drooped over sadly to the side, with mine still untouched. I fight back a shiver, the urge to leave this place and take her home with nothing to show for our day but her half-finished, slumped over bowl-like thing growing stronger and stronger by the minute.

"Hm. Careful, or you'll put ideas in my head."

"What if that's the goal?"

Lydia smiles up at me, bright and warm and seductive, and I feel it; My chest tightens with want and adoration and *love*. The realization that it's love, real and tangible, threatens to topple me, to knock me down and bring me to my knees. There's nothing I want to do more than to beg for her to just *love me back*.

I am completely, hopelessly in love with Lydia Michaelson. And I know, now, that there's no way for me to stop it, even if I wanted to.

Chapter 15

Lydia

When we leave the pottery studio, I want nothing more than to get my hands on Beck. Once we finally get back to the house, I don't waste any time. I kiss him hard. It's full of tenderness, slow and deliberate, like neither of us have ever done this before with each other. Beck takes his time with me, making sure that I feel every single movement of his hands, of his mouth, of *him* inside of me. He whispers sweet nothings against my skin, things for only he and I to know. Beck knows my body. Knows what to do to make me tick, knows how to bring me right to the edge over and over again.

Being with him is bliss.

I know that we're not done for the night, but once he's brought both me *and* him crashing to the edge, we lay together, tangled in his sheets and in each other. I don't think I have ever been this happy. Beck cards his hands through my hair lazily, looking at me like I'm something to be adored.

"What's something that you've never told me before?" Beck asks after we've been quiet for a few moments, shifting so that I'm lying beside him instead of on top of him. "Something that I wouldn't know about you?"

"Okay, that's hard." I say, chewing on the inside of my cheek as I think. "I think you know pretty much everything."

"Surely there's something."

A lot can change in three years. I know that much based solely on my own experience. Like divorce. Like questioning your career path. Like seeing your sister get engaged. All of this, though, Beck does already know.

"Actually, there might be something," I chime in, laughter already rising in me at how *stupid* what I'm about to say is.

"What is it?"

"Well. I have, like, a totally irrational fear of wet paper."

"Wet paper?" Beck blinks twice, tilting his head to the side like a confused little puppy.

Lydia: "Yeah."

"What is there to fear?"

"Maybe fear isn't the right word. It's disgusting. Utterly grotesque. Make me gag sort of stuff." Sitting up in bed excitedly. I prop myself up against the headboard, counting out all of the terrible incidents that I know on my fingers as I say them. "Spit wads. Disgusting. The way the paper will tear when it's too wet. Gag. Especially in public restrooms when there is wet toilet paper on the floor." I shudder in disgust. Just talking about it makes me want to vomit.

"This feels personal."

"Well, it *is* personal. I don't tell anyone for fear that they might find my revulsion amusing."

"Right, because someone might shoot spit wads at you."

"Be nice."

"I'm sorry," Beck says, sitting up beside me and pressing a kiss to my cheek. Even though he's being sweet, he still wears a chastising grin. But I can't fight back the smile that appears on my face when he's looking at me like that. "That actually does sound pretty overwhelming."

"What about you, then? What freaks you out? Surely, you're not just an impenetrable fortress, right? *Something* has to scare you."

"Well. There is something."

"Tell me." I turn to face him, sitting crisscross and propping my elbows up on my knees, my chin in my hands. Beck's expression clues me in, his twisted brow and pursed lips telling me that whatever this thing is really *does* freak him out.

"I'm completely terrified of the uncanny valley."

"What, now?" He waves me off, letting out a sigh and slumping further under the covers.

"This is how I know you're not into horror. The uncanny valley. Things that are almost human but are slightly off, so they feel like a threat." Even though I've never heard of it before, I get goosebumps from the description alone.

"Oh my God, what? That sounds horrible."

"Yeah, it's pretty... It's a tough one."

"How did you even find out that was something to be afraid of?"

"Like I said, I can tell that you're not into horror. It's a pretty popular fear to tap into nowadays," He explains, "Like *Us*. Jordan Peele's movie. That's kind of the uncanny valley, in a sense."

"That is *so* not the same thing as my revulsion to wet paper."

"It also means that I hate mannequins." Beck is a big man, but even *he* shivers when he says this.

"Oh. Yikes. Okay, I kind of get it."

"It's your turn to come up with a question now, though." Leaning towards me, he wraps his arms around my waist, pulling me back into his side.

"I just asked you one!"

"It was a follow-up to mine. Doesn't count. You have to ask me an original question."

"Fine. Okay," I start, humming slightly and drumming my fingers on his thigh as I think. "When did you decide to grow your hair out?" For all of the years I've known him, he's always kept his hair short; Now, his curly blond hair dips below his chin, making him look like some painting of a Greek god.

"Uh…" Scratching the side of his face, Beck takes his time to answer. "Probably right after the funeral."

I pause, my hand stilling on his thigh.

"Oh."

"Yeah. *Oh.*"

He wears that same wry grin on his face that tells me that he would rather *not* be remembering the thing he's thinking about. I don't blame him, though — that funeral was a living hell for him.

Heather's visitation was the last time that we saw each other before I got divorced. Beck was twenty pounds thinner, cheekbones sallow and eyes dark. I remember how shocking he looked juxtaposed against a backdrop of floral arrangements, lilies and carnations and all of the beautiful things draining his color even further. He wasn't even recognizable.

Heather's death was a stab to the gut. Seeing the way it almost killed Beck was a twist of the knife.

I hadn't gotten to stay long, mostly because of Tristan. In a way, I'm glad that I didn't have to stay there with him like that, watching him become a shell of himself, but I will also *never* be able to forgive Tristan for pulling me away during a time where I should have been grieving.

"Beck," I notice the shake in my voice before I notice how tight my throat feels. "I'm… I don't think I ever really got to talk to you about this, but I'm just so sorry. About Heather. About everything." He gives me a sad smile.

"You really don't have to apologize."

"I know, but I should've... I should've been there. Should've been more present for Amber *and* for you."

"Dee. You did everything you could," He reassures me, placing his hand on top of mine where it still sat on his leg. His blue eyes look glassy with the threat of tears, and it makes the lump in my throat just *that* much harder to swallow. "It's okay."

"We don't have to talk about this if you don't want to," I manage, shaking my head.

"No, I want to."

"Well." A shaky inhale. I steel myself for the question. "How has it been for you?

Since... since the accident?"

Beck is quiet for a moment. If I didn't know the way his mind worked, I would think that he's studying me. But I *do*, and so I know that Beck Shepherd is careful with his words. He knows the weight that they carry, he always has, so I'm sure that he's turning things over and over again in his mind, parsing through and sifting out *exactly* the right thing to say. To console me *and* to process it himself. He places his free hand on my cheek, caressing it gently with his thumb, before he speaks.

"At first, I was... I was numb. Catatonic, almost. Like I was sleepwalking through life. I know that the stages of grief aren't linear, but for the entire first *month*, it was like I felt all of it at once. Denial that I would never see her again. Anger that she left. Bargaining with any force that could hear me to bring her back and take me instead. Depression that kept me anchored to my bed for days on end. It was all... it was all swirling around in me like a storm that I couldn't quiet." He swallows harshly, then, and continues.

"When you get married, you say 'until death'. You assume that 'until death' means you'll be lying in bed with that person when you're old and pass together peacefully in your sleep. You don't ever imagine your spouse is going to die before you even reach your five-year anniversary." I don't even realize that I've started to cry until I feel Beck's other hand on my face, his thumbs gently stroking my tears away. That sad smile remains on his face, but he doesn't cry. He cried all of the tears that he needed to. I can tell based on his unwavering expression. Now, he's in the acceptance stage.

"I let myself be directionless, for a while," He admits. "I had hookups that went nowhere.

I was a regular at this one bar downtown, to the point where they knew my order. I lost myself. If I didn't have Amber, if I didn't have my support system, I don't know where I would be. I don't know if I ever would have gotten out of it. But I did."

"I'm glad you did," My voice is barely above a whisper as I sniff, turning my head into one of his hands and pressing a gentle kiss to his palm. "I don't know what... I don't know what I would have done if something had happened to you." Beck's face softens immediately, and he shakes his head, pressing his lips to my forehead gently.

"You don't have to think about that. I'm here. And I'm okay now." Another small kiss to my forehead, and then he pulls me into his chest, hugging me close and placing his chin on top of my head. "Acceptance didn't come for me until *way* later. I don't even remember it being a conscious thing. I just... I remember telling someone that I was a widower, getting a sympathetic look, and that was that. I didn't feel the need to run from it. And I know that pottery helped me get through it. Helped me channel all of my feelings into something creative and productive."

"I'm so proud of you," I say into his chest, and I mean it with every fiber of my being.

"And I miss her. Of course I miss her. Every day. But what I've realized is that..." He pauses, then, pulling away to look me in the eyes. There's the smallest of creases between his brows, hinting at nervousness. "What I've realized is that Heather would have wanted me to be happy. She wouldn't have wanted me to spend my whole life missing her. And Lydia? Lydia, *you* make me happy."

I feel my heart skip a beat. I'm almost not processing the words he's saying, staring at him blankly and trying not to burst into tears.

"What?" Beck scoots closer to me, then, his hands on my shoulders, his earnest expression and the softness in his voice making me melt.

"This. Us. *You.* This trip is the happiest I've been... God, in a long fucking time." He laughs dryly as he says it, and a tear finally rolls down his cheek. "I don't want to freak you out. I don't want to put any pressure on you or on this. But I just... There's something here, right? It's not just me?"

For a moment, I'm quiet. I don't want to burst this bubble; don't want to ruin whatever thing it is that we have going on. Whatever world we're living in here, on this vacation. I know that he's being genuine, I know that he wouldn't just say this on a whim — He's never been the type. So, I face my fears of vulnerability, letting myself be *seen* for the moment by Beck Shepherd.

"No. No, it's not just you."

I kiss him. I kiss him like I mean it, like it's the last time anyone will ever kiss someone on the Earth. And I come to the startling realization, then, that I am falling deeply, *hopelessly* in love.

Chapter 16

Beck

Even though this isn't by any means the first time Lydia and I have kissed, it feels like it is. My heart pounds in my chest until I think I could explode. It's like this every time — there's something about being with her that undoes me, even with the most subtle forms of intimacy.

But this time, everything feels less rushed. Every movement of her lips against mine is intentional. Her hands push against my shoulders so that we roll over, and I'm on top of her, pressing my full body weight against her. I can't think of anything but Lydia, can't bring myself to break this kiss even if my life depended on it.

To me, she's the only woman who has ever existed. And I intend to show her that.

My hands travel up her sides underneath her shirt, and she arches her back up with my touch. I want her to feel all of it, down to her core, for her to know that each touch is conveying what I actually feel about her. I love you. You don't know that yet, but I've known it forever. I love you, and I feel like I always will.

My hands find her breasts, and I give them a light squeeze over the cloth of her bra. This earns me a contented moan; Lydia gasps into my open mouth as she pulls back for air, and the intimacy of the gesture makes me weak.

"You're so beautiful," I mumble against her lips, feeling my way around to her back. I unclasp her bra in one smooth motion, and then my hands are back on her, massaging her breast with my left and pinching her nipple between my thumb and forefinger with my right. "So, fucking beautiful."

"Beck," Lydia gasps, her fists tugging at my curls, "More."

I don't hesitate. Wrapping my arms around her torso, I lift her so that she's sitting upright, shimmying her shirt over her head for her. She's looking at me wide-eyed, like she's never been touched like this before, and I'm about to fall apart. I pull my own shirt over my head, and we sit there like that for a moment, panting and catching our breath.

Moving both of my hands to cup her face gently, I run my thumbs across her cheekbone, memorizing her face in the moonlight. I can't believe that she's real — she's the most beautiful thing I've ever seen. And I will give up anything and everything to stay like this forever.

Our lips collide again, and I pull her into my lap. Lydia wraps her legs around my waist eagerly, our torsos pressing together. All of her soft curves are flush against me, and I press her body against my own even more vigorously, before I move to litter kisses down her neck. She gasps softly, and tilts her head to give me more access. When I start to suck and nibble at the divot where her neck meets her shoulder, she whimpers softly, rolling her hips against mine eagerly. The friction is exactly what I need, my cock already straining against the fabric of my underwear. The thin boundary doesn't provide much separation, though, and the warmth of her core against me as she grinds makes me feel almost feral.

"That's it, baby," I mumble against her skin, letting out a low groan as I rock my hips up into hers, "Good girl. Make yourself feel good." And then she lets out a little noise of pleasure as her forehead falls against my shoulder, rutting her hips into mine with even more intensity. As she grinds into me with each thrust, I can feel the precum starting to soak through the fabric of my boxers, and a slick trail of her own wetness gathering at her center. Each time she moves her hips, she does so a little harder, and I try to angle my hips to make it easier for her to rub herself just there on her clit, the way I know she likes it.

"Beck, oh my God," Lydia gasps, a little whine falling from her lips as her movements increase in speed. "Need you. Fuck. Please, I'm close." I almost feel bad for denying her an orgasm, but I want to bring her right to that edge, just to see how far she's willing to push herself. When I shift our bodies again, pinning her down underneath me and effectively stunting her movements, she whines in protest, before I roll my hips against hers one more time for good measure.

"Sorry, sweetheart," I say, my voice rough and low, "But I need to feel you clenching around me when you come for the first time tonight. Hips up, please." This seems to satiate her, at least for the moment, and so I hook my fingers around the waistband of her panties, pulling them down past her hips and making quick work to kick off my boxers.

Looking at Lydia underneath me, golden brown hair splayed out across the pillow with a look of pure want on her face, I am completely convinced that I will never be able to get over seeing her like this. She looks like something out of a renaissance painting, like one of those women that men would have gone to war for. I am certain that now that I've had a glimpse of her like this, now that I've developed a taste for her, that I will crave seeing her exactly like this for the rest of my life.

And the thought doesn't scare me. If anything, it makes me want her that much more, makes me want to prove myself to her every day. To prove my love to her here and now, like this, our bodies pressed together in an act of pure devotion.

"You ready?" I ask her gently, brushing a strand of hair out of her face so that I can see her better. Lydia nods, and I push into her, groaning as my entire length slips in, all the way to the hilt.

"Holy fuck," I hiss, stilling for a moment once I'm fully seated inside, "You feel so good."

"Beck," She whines, her tone breathless and pleading as she tries to grind her hips down further into mine. "Beck, I need to feel you move. Need you to fill me over and over again."

How could I do anything but oblige when asked so sweetly? Without hesitation, I start to roll my hips, almost painstakingly slowly at first. I want her to feel every movement, and I gasp a little bit every time I do it, the sensation almost completely overwhelming for me. I want this to last forever. No, I need it to.

It's a test of my endurance to keep going so slowly, at first. A test at how patient I can be, how far I can stretch myself so that I'm making this experience as raw and meaningful and real for her as possible. And then I watch as Lydia's hand dips down to her center, circling her clit in time with my thrusts. I groan in delicious pleasure at the sight of it, the idea that she's pleasuring herself as I'm fucking her almost more than I can bear. I pick up the pace, then, watching in fevered devotion as she continues circling her fingers to match my thrusts.

"God, you look so good like that, Lydia," I gasp, and she opens her eyes into mine, then — our gazes locked, I let out a groan that is almost inhuman, my hands gripping her waist as my fingertips dig into her hips. I feel myself teetering closer and closer to the edge with each thrust and with each word of encouragement that falls from her lips. She continuously chants declarations of how good this is for her and how good of a job I'm doing in a way that makes me feel like I'm the only man who's ever touched her.

And if I'm doing my job right, she'll forget any other man ever has.

"Close," She gasps after another moment, her fingers circling her clit more rapidly now.

A fervor that's only matched by my own thrusts.

"Come on, baby," I manage through gritted teeth, "Come around my cock. Need to see that pretty face when you finish."

"Fuck!" Lydia cries out, her eyes snapping closed as she circles her fingers more diligently, her breath coming in smaller and smaller gasps. "Fuck, I'm gonna—"

Her walls clench around me, pulsing and tightening as she reaches her peak. Between the noises that she makes as she's finishing and the sensation of her pleasure adding just another amount of pressure to my cock, I'm falling apart inside of her with a cry, my entire load filling her up and coating her walls in thick streaks. I say her name like it's a swear as I ride us both out through our respective highs, my thrusts becoming sloppier and less intentional as I rut into her instinctively.

"Jesus," I finally say, gasping for air as my thrusts slow. I collapse on top of her, then, completely spent, but still fully seated inside. "God, you're amazing." I kiss her, then, and she kisses back greedily, hands fisted against my chest.

When we break for air, she beams up at me, cheeks flushed and lips swollen. I want to be greedy, want to kiss her again over and over until we're no longer two separate people. And it hits me, then, that I would do anything and everything this woman asked me to.

And I don't want to rush it, don't want to push her into anything she's not ready for. So I hold her, kissing her skin ever so gently, and hope beyond all reason that by some miracle, she feels the same way that I do.

That maybe, just maybe, Lydia loves me too.

Chapter 17

Lydia

For some indiscernible reason, I'm awake. I don't know if I had caffeine too late, or if the high from being with Beck is just that potent. It's well past midnight, though, and I'm scrolling aimlessly on my phone, filling my mind with recipes that I'll tell myself I'll remember and opinions about a celebrity scandal that I can take back to work and talk about in the break room.

Typically, I don't have trouble falling asleep. I have a routine, and it works — I wash my face and do my skincare, brush my teeth, turn on my Spotify sleep timer and play brown noise while I count sheep. Probably I could have done that tonight, but watching Beck fall asleep had been more of a priority for me. I wanted to memorize him; The way his eyelashes fluttered closed, the snoring that was actually soft enough to be endearing rather than annoying, the little curls that stayed plastered firmly to his forehead. He looked so peaceful, and so many years younger, like the Beck that I'd been kids with once. It felt like forever ago and just yesterday all at once, seeing him that way — just a little boy with saltwater dripping from his shaggy curls, face covered in freckles and touting a bit of a sunburn.

I wish it could be that simple again, but I know that wishing for that is an empty hope. There's so much that we've been through, together and apart, and life won't ever be that simple again.

How am I supposed to reconcile that, though, when his face looks exactly how it did back

then?

12:30 AM. I'm almost too lost in my own train of thought to see the notification appear along the top of my phone screen.

New iMessage — from Tristan

This can't be good.

For a moment, I consider swiping out of it. Consider opening up the messages app and deleting our text conversation, but then I see a photo in the corner of the message and a vague impression of a palm tree in the background. Puzzled, I click on the message.

The picture is a selfie of Tristan and I, nearly 10 years ago now when we went on our honeymoon. I recognize it immediately, because he'd told me some crass jokes beforehand and gotten me to laugh. My face is a little blurry and I'm turning towards him to bury my face in his shoulder, embarrassed by the purposefully goofy face he's pulling at the camera.

At the time, I didn't think I'd ever laughed so hard in my life. A pang of guilt rushes through me. I don't know why, I can't place it.

We were just kids.

My thoughts are finally interrupted again by the phone buzzing in my hand. Tristan.

Incoming Call. I should let it ring. I should let it go to voicemail.

But, then again, I feel like I need to give him a piece of my mind. It's not fair for him to keep bringing up these memories. They're all stained now.

As quietly as I can, I clamber out of bed, stepping outside and closing the door with a little click behind me. I take a deep breath, and then I answer.

"Tristan, what is this?" I ask him point-blank, trying to keep my volume as low as possible. "Why are you calling?"

"It's from our honeymoon," Tristan says, and the fluidity and unsteadiness of his words clue me in. He's drunk. Again . "You remember? In St. Lucia." I don't even want to dignify that question with a response. I sigh heavily, shaking my head and pressing my palm to my forehead in frustration, even though he can't see me.

"Yes, I remember St. Lucia," I say after a moment, "But that doesn't answer my question.

Why are you calling?"

"Take me back, Lydia."

The weight of his words threaten to topple me. Not once in the entirety of our divorce proceedings, in the weeks and months leading up to the finalization had he asked me this. I almost want to think that I'm dreaming it all.

"I'm sorry," I start, laughing humorlessly as I pace the hallway. "I think I just hallucinated. What? "

I don't even realize I'm quoting Legally Blonde until the words have passed my lips. He wouldn't know this, though, but apparently, even my sleep-deprived brain still finds ways to bring up Elle Woods at inopportune moments.

"I asked you to take me back," He presses on, "I'm sick of pretending I don't love you. Sick of us fighting. Sick of checking the listing for our home and trying to imagine what it looked like before you emptied it out like that. Before you gutted the entire place." There's no sugar-coating it. Tristan sounds miserable. But the accusations he throws at me that are sandwiched between his pleas only harden me further, bolstering my anger. Until my resentment for him is a knife, sharp and violent.

"Oh, how sad," I say, though my voice is devoid of any real pity. "Maybe if you paid attention while you lived there, maybe if you weren't drunk out of your mind every single night, you wouldn't have such a difficult time remembering."

"That's a low fucking blow, Lydia, and you know it."

"Alright. Then tell me I'm wrong. Tell me you're not drunk right now."

"I'm not." Every word he says runs together like water. I can't help but laugh.

"Liar."

"I'm not !" The way he raises his voice at me still makes me jump. And I remember, then, exactly why I left him in the first place. Any thoughts of softness that I had towards him after seeing that photo of us are quickly erased, gone as if they'd never even been there to begin with.

"Oh, I'm so sorry. That's my mistake," My voice is as emotionally vacant as I am. "Have you been going to acting classes, then? Because you're definitely putting on a really good drunk man impression right now."

"Funny, I was gonna ask you the same thing. Your raging bitch impression has improved." His words feel like a snap to the face. It always did when he cursed at me, but bitch is actually a new one for him, and it stings.

It hits me, then, that I've always been the calm one. I've always been the one to be cool and collected in elevated moments, or I've retreated inward.

But now, I don't have to worry about him. He doesn't own me. I am my own person.

And I can fight back.

" Fuck you," I hiss, seething. Years of resentment and bitterness embolden me, fuelling me with a righteous kind of anger that I didn't even know I was capable of. Then, Tristan laughs at me, and the sound of it makes me nauseous.

"You wish."

"I would rather die."

"Wasn't always the case." Even though I know he can't see me, I roll my eyes. It's incredible how he can still manage to get on my nerves from thousands of miles away.

"Tristan, I'm not continuing this conversation." I try to sound as stern as possible, try to make myself come across as someone who is not to be messed with. As someone who isn't going

to continue to let her ex-husband walk all over her. "There isn't any point. I'm not coming back to you."

"And why not?" I scoff at the fact that he even has to ask, and I don't even hesitate before I let the words that I know will crush him come flying out of my mouth.

"Because I met someone else."

I don't even realize what this implies in regards to my own feelings about Beck. When I say it, I catch a glimpse of myself in the hallway mirror. As resolute as I try to convince myself I am, I definitely don't look as unyielding as I feel. My hair is a mess and my eyes are bloodshot. I might as well be a character on The Walking Dead.

I haven't explored what Beck really is to me beyond our surface-level attraction. I know that I meant what I said to him, that there was something more than just physical attraction, but it's been so long since I've been in this... newer stage of things with someone, that I feel like I'm on unsteady footing.

Without a doubt, though, I know this will get under Tristan's skin. I want to get out of this conversation, and he doesn't have to know all the details. All I need to do is rub it in a little, make him think that there really is something going on, and if all goes according to plan, he'll leave me alone.

"You what ?" Suddenly, he sounds almost alarmingly sober. It's unsettling.

"I met someone else, Tristan. I'm... I'm seeing someone, okay? That's all you get to know."

"What do you mean you're seeing someone? Our divorce has been final for, what, a month?"

"Like you haven't slept with anything that walks at those bars that you've been to." His hypocrisy is laughable. We both know he's lying to himself and to me, and I can tell he's angry when he groans in frustration.

"That's not the same!" He cries, but he doesn't deny he's seen people since the divorce. Point proven. I want to gloat, but he doesn't give me the chance. "You're telling me that you're in a relationship , Lydia. You have to admit that it's crazy. You have to admit that it's fast."

"I didn't say relationship."

"That's what you implied!"

"Listen. I don't have to explain anything to you," At this point, I'm pacing back and forth in the narrow hallway. I keep catching uncomfortable glances of myself in the dark. I'm running my hands through my messy hair incessantly, an unconscious manifestation of my anxiety. "I don't owe you anything—"

"So who is he?" Tristan pointedly cuts me off before I can finish my thought, and I'm in disbelief that this is what he's now choosing to focus on.

"What?"

"Who is he?" He sounds like he's either about to cry or scream at me until I can't think. "Surely he's not some stranger, surely you knew him before this. You're too careful to jump into something blind like that. I mean, hell, when we first started dating, you sat me down and interviewed me before we even went out for the first time."

"You don't know that!" I don't know why I'm trying to argue with him about this. Maybe it's because I feel like I know how he's going to feel about the actual answer to his question.

"I've changed! I can be spontaneous!"

"No, you can't. Now who is it?"

"I don't have to tell you anything. Oh my God. I'm hanging up."

"It's Shepherd, isn't it?"

Silence is the only thing that crackles over the line. There's no way that he guessed it that easily, right? I didn't even... didn't even think about Beck that way until we came on this trip. I had no idea that he thought about me that way either. It never even seemed like an option. Beck was always more popular than me, was always on sports teams and was homecoming king and I was just a dorky AP and Honors student.

But even still, Tristan had been jealous of our friendship when we started dating. I'd had to talk him down from the ledge so many times, and had to convince him that I really didn't feel anything for Beck at all. And I meant it at the time. But it still took a lot of time to try and get

Tristan to believe me.

Now, it's occurring to me that maybe, he never fully did.

Maybe that's what drove Beck and I apart for all those years. Maybe it was a subtle play on his part, since he couldn't stand the fact that I was friends with someone that threatened his ego. I realize that I've been silent for long enough for Tristan to come up with the answer on his own when he curses.

"I fuckin' knew it." I hear a glass shatter in the background, and then he curses more. I wonder what he broke, for a moment, and hope that maybe it was alcohol that he can now no longer drink.

"Tristan, stop," I manage. For some reason, I'm starting to get choked up, and I briefly hate myself for letting him do this to me. For letting him get the reaction that he wants.

"All this time, and all you wanted to do was get rid of me to live out your little fantasy with perfect Beck Shepherd—"

"Stop—"

"I mean, I bet you were already fucking him before the divorce was even final—" The tears of frustration are cascading down my cheeks faster than I can wipe them away.

"Tristan, please—" My voice breaks when I say this, and I know he can tell that I'm crying. That he thinks he won.

"But you were never what he wanted. You know that, right?" Tristan sounds nearly gleeful. With every word, he's stomping on my heart, sending me into a spiral of overthinking and anxiety. I hate that he knows exactly the right things to say to get me to break, to get me to crack. If I were a stronger person, maybe I wouldn't let him affect me this way.

But I'm not that person. And I feel so, so incredibly small because of it.

"I bet he's just sad about his wife," He slurs, "That he's just doing you and pretending that you're her because he hasn't slept with anyone in years—"

"Stop it—"

"Is he at least good? I mean, being celibate for three years will really take a toll on you. He's nothing, Lydia. He's just some person at a desk job who won't be able to give you anywhere near as much financial freedom as we had when we were married. You can kiss your fancy little trips goodbye—"

"Stop! Stop, stop, stop!" My pleas fall on deaf ears. I have to bite my fist to keep myself from screaming.

"Oh, I'm sorry, was I too brutally honest for you? Did I hurt your feelings?"

"I hate you," I sob.

"That's rich, Lydia. That's completely fucking rich. You don't hate me, not even a little.

You wanna know how I know?"

At this point, my voice is weak. Small. I haven't been able to think straight for the entirety of this conversation; I have fallen down a spiral of self-hatred, one that's mostly of my own creation. I know I'm not going to win this fight. Tristan is a master manipulator, and I just happen to be a victim of his actions. After a long beat of silence, I take an unsteady breath, wiping my eyes with the back of my sleeve.

"How?"

"Because if you did hate me, you wouldn't answer my calls."

He hangs up, the line going dead. I can't breathe. I press my back against the wall and sink down to the ground, sobbing into my hands.

How pathetic do I have to be to be crying like this over my ex-husband when there's an angel of a man in the next room? I feel nauseous, unable to lift my head and face the emptiness and darkness of the night. My chest clenches with the weight of all of the loathing and the uncertainty. And the worst part?

The worst part is that he's not entirely wrong.

We were tied to each other for years. Christmases, birthdays, Thanksgivings, the merging of families. It all hangs heavily over the decision to end a marriage, and I thought that I had gotten myself through it all. Thought that I had come to terms with all of it, that I knew we were better off apart. Thought I'd made peace with the fact that no matter how much history was there, that I couldn't and wouldn't keep subjecting myself to Tristan's temper.

Maybe the delusion of my acceptance was to cushion the blow of everything else. Maybe I couldn't handle processing the divorce, my career questions, and how far ahead of me that my friends all are in their lives all at once. Maybe I've just been kidding myself this entire time, fooling myself into believing that I am unaffected by everything.

I'm struck, then, with a startling fear; What if this is too soon? I did just get divorced. Less than a month ago. And now, here I am, letting myself get caught up in something with my best friend. With Beck .

And do I really know how Beck feels about it all? He said that there was something more than physical he felt, but what does that even mean? Was I just assuming it meant that he cared for me romantically, when he really could have meant anything?

I take in a few deep breaths in an attempt to calm myself down. In and out. In and out. But I can't shake it, the feeling that I've gotten myself too invested in something that I really shouldn't have. On some level, I know that I'm entering self-destruct mode, but lighting everything on fire and being the one to control the blaze seems far preferable to getting hurt by this.

When I finally calm myself down, I pick myself up off the floor and go to Amber's room alone.

Chapter 18

Beck

When I wake up, the side of the bed next to mine is cold.

This wouldn't have been a shock to me until a few days ago. Until this trip , actually. I'd gotten so used to sleeping alone that I hardly realized how easy it was to expect another body there again, another person. As I stretch out this morning, though, I expect to feel Lydia there, where she has been for the past few nights. When my arm is met with nothing, though, I'm immediately more awake than I was just a few moments prior, sitting up and rubbing the sleep out of my eyes as I look around the room.

The blankets on the right side of the bed are tossed to the side, haphazard evidence that she had actually been there in the first place. That I hadn't just dreamed the whole thing. But there isn't even an indentation in the pillow, so she can't have just gotten up.

It hits me, then, how strange it is that I'd been expecting her to be there in the first place.

We had only been seeing each other for a few days, after all. And I don't even know if I can be calling it that — it's not like we've given it a name, though, or an official title, so maybe there's no harm in it. Maybe she just got up to eat breakfast or make coffee or something and didn't want to wake me up. Which is fine.

If it's fine , though, as I continue to tell myself that it is, why am I unable to shake the feeling that something is wrong?

I grab a pair of sweats out of my dresser and put them on, before making my way downstairs. Lydia is, as I suspected, sitting in the kitchen at one of the four barstools. Relief fills me at the sight of her, but as I walk over to her, I realize that this relief may have been a little bit premature.

Usually, Lydia is a morning person. She manages to look like it, too, her eyes bright and her smile wide. Today, though, there's bags under her eyes, to the point where I wonder if she got any sleep at all. The bowl of cereal in front of her looks almost as though she's forgotten it as she scrolls absently on her phone, stirring it around and around, even though it's already reduced to mush.

"Woah," I say to her, trying to sound lighthearted, "Somebody looks like they need some coffee." Immediately after I say it, though, I notice that her cup of coffee is practically untouched and probably cold, sitting in front of her next to the cereal. I decide not to comment on this, though, and I walk up behind her.

When I wrap my arms around her, leaning in to try and kiss her cheek, I notice the slightest bit of resistance from her. It would be barely noticeable if I weren't so close to her, but she pulls away just a touch before stopping herself, and my brow furrows. She isn't acting like herself.

"Is... everything okay?" I ask after a moment, pulling back enough to study her expressions.

"Yeah." Lydia doesn't even look up from her phone when she says it. "Just didn't sleep well." Keep it light, Beck, I think, Maybe she got some bad news or something. Make a joke.

"Ah. Does my breath stink?" I ask with a chuckle, sliding my arms around her tighter. "I mean, I can go brush my teeth if that's what it is—"

"It's fine, Beck." Her words sound clipped. Harsh. She still doesn't look at me. I pause for a moment, then, pursing my lips and trying my best not to be irritated by how short she's being with me when I don't have any way of knowing what I've done. So, I pull away, moving to sit next to her at the counter instead, taking the stool next to hers so I can see her face more clearly. I study her expression. She's completely stoic, her face revealing nothing. Her leg bounces where it's propped on the rung of the chair.

"It doesn't seem fine."

"Listen, I'm okay ," Lydia says, the irritation clear in her tone as she finally looks up at me. Her voice is higher-pitched than it usually is. "I promise." Then, her voice barely above a whisper as she turns back to her phone: "I'm not even yours to worry about in the first place."

I almost don't think I heard her right. I'm not even yours to worry about in the first place.

The words are cutting and cruel and very unlike her. Silence hangs thick and heavy between us as I try (and fail) to process what it might mean. What she might be thinking. A humorless laugh bubbles past my lips.

Okay," I say plainly, cocking my head to one side, "What's that supposed to mean?" It's sharper than I intended for it to be.

"Nothing!" Immediately, she colors, her voice shrill. In clear agitation, she places her phone in her lap, fully turning to face me. "Just — it means nothing, okay? Can you drop it?"

"Lydia, you're not talking to me. I don't know how you expect me—"

"I don't expect you to do anything. Okay? There is nothing involving me that you are obligated to do."

"I... know that?"

"Okay, good." I can hear my heartbeat in my ears. I don't know what to feel or what to think. Clearly, she's angry at me, but had I done something? I try to parse through it all in my mind, trying to remember what had been said between us over the course of the past day that would give me any sort of clues. And then she's staring straight into the bowl of cereal, stirring it over and over again, the soggy cereal disintegrating in the milk.

"Okay. I'm confused," I say finally, breaking the silence and looking over at her pleadingly. I wish she would just tell me the answer, tell me what it is that I did to mess up so that we could go back to the way things were again.

"Confused?" She asks flatly. Trying to gather my thoughts, I chew on the inside of my cheek. I don't want to say the wrong thing or put my foot in my mouth.

"Why are you being so... so cold towards me all of a sudden?" Lydia lifts her eyes, furrowing her eyebrows at me in a look that could either mean Why are you being so dumb? Or I hate you. Clearly, I'd chosen the wrong words.

"I'm not?"

"No, you are," I say, pushing forward even in spite of everything I know about women telling me that I probably shouldn't be doing that.

"Beck, I—"

"I mean, after the other night," I say, leaning forward towards her, trying in a way that's almost desperate to get her to see my side of things. "After the... after I told you that there was something more —"

"A mistake."

Those words hit me like a blow to the chest. I lean back in my chair, stunned silent for a moment. Surely she doesn't mean it. Surely she's just angry, and I should have taken the hint and left her alone the first time.

Instead, like an idiot, I continue my tirade of questions.

"A mistake ?" I ask, dumbfounded.

"That was a mistake," Lydia responds, clearly doubling down on her stance. I feel sick when she says it. "I shouldn't have said that. Neither of us should have said that." Despite the harshness of her words, despite the resolution in her gaze, there's still a small shake in her voice. An uncertainty. Her eyes are glassy with the threat of tears, and to me, she doesn't look like someone who's convinced they shouldn't have done something. She just looks sad.

"I don't understand," I say after a moment, noticing the quiver in my own words.

"Oh, come on. Yes you do. This was... it's casual , right?" She gestures back and forth between the two of us with one hand. "We're being casual about this. There aren't any strings attached. No one's feelings are going to get involved, because we're adults. We can handle this like adults. We can sleep together, and that's fine, but we both knew that this would be over by the time we got home, anyway."

"Is that really how you feel?" I feel my temper threatening to flare, and I resist the urge to ask her if it's me she's trying to convince of that fact or herself.

"This isn't real life, Beck!" Lydia snaps. A tear rolls down her cheek, and as badly as I want to reach out to her, want to wipe it away, I stop myself. Because what she is saying hurts , and I am stubborn and feeling a hot rush of new anger rising in my core with every single word. "This is a fantasy. This is a vacation. We're kidding ourselves if we think that we're going to magically be able to, I don't know, continue whatever it is we're doing once we get back home. I have a career, a life, a house that I need to focus on selling."

"Right. So that's all this has been to you this whole time? Some sort of game? Some... some little hookup to get your mind off your divorce?" The words come out of my mouth before I can stop myself. I regret it instantly, but even though she looks deeply hurt by this, I don't back down. I should back down, but every single word she says drives a stake through my heart, crushing all of my dreams of what could have been with her.

"Beck, that is so unfair."

"Oh, I'm the one who's being unfair?"

"By using my divorce against me? Painting me as someone who would take advantage of you like that? That's a low blow."

"Actions speak louder than words, you know. I think you might be the one who painted yourself as someone who would do that." My voice comes out more harshly than I intended. I don't mean to raise my voice at her, but I do. The way she looks at me, though, is something I've never seen before — a look of genuine shock and deep hurt, of betrayal and heartache. Her lip quivers as more tears roll down her cheeks.

Even though I'm hurt, I feel absolutely terrible for having made her feel this way. I take a deep breath; I can't let my anger control me. I know too well how much of that she already dealt with. I can only imagine the myriad of things Tristan would say to her in the heat of an argument. Hurting her or making her lose trust in me in any way is the last thing that I want to do, and the guilt that builds and plateaus inside me mingles with my own feelings of heartbreak.

Because I feel hurt. I feel taken advantage of. I feel lied to and used.

"Right. Okay. So we can't be adults about this, can we? Good to know." Lydia moves to stand, wiping her eyes with the back of her sleeve as she does so. I stand, too, running a frustrated hand through my hair.

"I guess not. Not since feelings got involved —"

"Oh, now you want to talk to me about feelings ?" She snaps, and she laughs at me. It's cold and cutting, and completely devoid of any humor. I feel myself crumbling underneath it.

"That's ridiculous. You're ridiculous, Beck."

"Sure. Fine. I'm ridiculous," I grit out through clenched teeth, trying my best to swallow down the rising tide of my own emotion. "I'm out of my mind, I'm completely insane, aren't I?

Because I'm in love with a girl who hasn't ever loved me back and who clearly will never love me back." I taste the salt of my tears on my cheek before I even realize I'm crying.

"Don't do that," Lydia sobs, backing away from me. I try to walk towards her, but she shakes her head.

"Lydia, please. Please listen to me, I mean it, I love you—"

"No! You don't get to do that. Not now. That's not okay, Beck." Before I know it, she's headed towards the door, grabbing the keys to my family's Jeep off the hook by the door. This can't be happening. She can't be leaving. Not like this.

But she is leaving. I barely catch up to her at the door before she swings it open, not even bothering to turn around and spare me a parting glance.

"Wait, Lydia. Lydia, please. Where are you going?"

"Anywhere but here."

"Lydia, please, stop—" I grab her arm to try and stop her, but she yanks herself out of my grasp, stopping me harshly as she finally turns to face me.

"No. I can't..." She takes in a shaky breath. "I can't do this right now. Okay? You've said enough. So just let me go. You... I just can't even look at you right now, Beck."

She storms out, slamming the door behind her.

I stare at the place where she had just been, dumbfounded. The sound of the Jeep cranking and the tires squealing out of the driveway don't even get me to budge. I'm frozen in place. Should I chase after her? Should I run down the road like I'm crazy?

But I'm rooted in place. I don't know what just happened. A few hours ago, I was ready to tell her that I wanted to take her on a date. Wanted to treat her the way she deserved to be treated, wanted to make this thing real for the both of us. And now?

Now, the girl I love is gone, and I'm to blame.

I don't know how long I stand there. I watch clouds crowd the sky, hear thunder crash and see lightning illuminate the sky, the sun completely obscured. The rain comes down, then, hard and unrelenting, and I finally snap myself out of whatever trance I'd been in.

Without even realizing I'd made the decision to do so, I pick up my phone to call my sister. The line rings twice, and then stops short of a third when Amber answers.

"Beckster! Hey! How's the trip going?" Her tone is cheerful as ever. "Are you guys—"

"Lydia just left."

"Wait, I'm sorry, what ?"

"She left. I fucked it up, and she left."

Static crackles across the line. I'm assuming that my sister is trying to process things, and I hear her whispering something along the lines of I don't know, he sounds upset to Melanie, who I know is probably able to hear everything I'm saying.

"Okay," She finally says, taking in a sharp breath, "I'm confused. I'm going to need a little bit of context, please."

So, I tell her everything. I try to fight back the tears, but to no avail. My voice is hoarse from crying, and I'm slumped against the door, staring vacantly into the empty and far too quiet living room as I recount it all. The initial hookup. How we'd been unable to keep ourselves away from each other when we got here. How I'd realized over the course of the trip that I really do love her, that she's the only person that I want to share all of this with anymore. And, of course, my miraculous way of fucking it all up. Once I've told her everything, once I've told her every terrible thing I said to Lydia to get her to leave, Amber heaves a sigh that I can only interpret as meaning Beck, you idiot.

"I can't believe neither of you said anything to me about this. It's been going on since

Callaghan's? "

"That's entirely besides the point, Amber."

"But still —"

" Amber ."

"Okay, jeez," My sister groans, and I hear the sound of shuffling in the background and the sound of a closing door. "Well, I mean, you know you messed up, right?"

"Yeah, that's pretty obvious."

"Okay, so you just need to give her time and then you can apologize. If I had to guess, the whole reason she got upset in the first place is because Tristan was probably being an asshole to her."

I can't believe it took me until my sister said it to figure it out. Of course . Of course he got in her head. Of course he freaked her out. I should have realized.

"I don't even know where to start with that, Amber." I rub the back of my neck anxiously as another flash of lightning shoots through the sky. "I don't even know where she is. I don't know if she's okay or not."

"You have to give it time, Beck. You can't just force it. You guys are going to be okay." I want to laugh at the incredulity of that statement. Want to tell her she has no idea what she's talking about, want to hang up the phone and hurl it across the room and scream. But I fight against that instinct, taking in a shaky breath as I finally find the right words.

"How can you be so sure?" I ask, and Amber doesn't hesitate. Her answer is immediate and sure, like it's a statement of fact.

"Because you two are meant to be, Beck."

Chapter 19

Lydia

I'm at the airport by 4 A.M.

I had decided to catch the next red eye home when I left Beck's house. I can't even really remember what I did for most of the day — I just drove and sat on the beach and drove some more while I cried. I had to go back to the house to get my things, too, and luckily, Beck wasn't there when I went. Once everything was shoved in my suitcase and the Jeep keys were back in their proper place, I called the most expensive Uber of my life to drive me to the hotel I'd booked for the night that was directly across the street from the airport. The hotel I slept at was barely a hotel; I suppose by definition it would be called a motel, since the entrances were outside. Fittingly, though, I barely slept at the place that was barely a hotel. The bed was uncomfortable, and the shower had been lukewarm, and I stared at the ceiling, trying to produce tears that just wouldn't come.

I ruined my chance with Beck. That, I know for sure.

The note I had left for Beck when I went back to the house for my things told him where I was going and that I was sorry. There were so many things that I wanted to say, so many details that I wanted to try to explain, but I wasn't able to find the words.

So, sleep deprived and bleary-eyed, I make my way to my flight. And once I'm in the air, safely hurdling away from all of the mistakes that I'm now so desperate to leave behind, I'm finally able to rest.

It's barely a wink of sleep, though, as I wake up with a jolt once we touch down. Where am I? Then I remember — the fight, the plane. The flight that I'm supposed to be on tomorrow that Amber paid for already. Racked with guilt for my impulsivity, I Venmo Amber what I expect to be more than the cost of one of the plane tickets with no explanation (once my phone is off airplane mode, that is). I'm sure she'll call me eventually and question what's going on, but it's still early enough in the morning that I know she's definitely still asleep.

We land, I go to baggage claim, and I call my sister. She answers on the first ring and is on her way within five minutes.

I'm standing outside by the pick-up zone by my gate, and as soon as I see Olivia's car rounding the corner, the tears that I'd been trying to hold back cascade down my face.

"Hey, Dee," she says gently as she rolls down the window, the small hint of a smile on her face fading instantly as soon as she recognizes my distress. "Oh gosh, honey. Come here."

Olivia steps out of the car, then, walking over to me and throwing her arms around me in a protective hug. All at once, I'm a little girl again, crying into my big sister's shoulder after a scraped knee. I hold onto her like she's my only anchor. We stand there for a long time, and she rubs comforting circles into my back. Finally, once my sobbing has subsided into a steadier cry, Olivia pulls away, both of her hands on my shoulders.

"Are you okay?" She asks me, and I nod. Of course, I'm not okay, but I don't actively need her to be hugging me anymore, which is what she meant by her question. "Here, you don't have to say anything," Olivia continues, "Let me get your bags." As she walks around to grab my luggage from behind me, I wipe my eyes and my nose and my entire face, trying to regain my composure. Once she's done putting them in the trunk, she crosses back to me for another hug.

I'm thankful she does, until I hear the sound of a man's throat clearing behind me.

"Excuse me, ma'am?" The voice continues, and I feel my sister's gaze shift to the person behind us, "You can't park here." He must be airport security. My sister tries to wave him off.

"We're not going to be long," Olivia says in an attempt to reassure him, "She's just having a little bit of a hard time." A beat passes, and for a moment, I think the person must have left. But we must not be that lucky.

"I really need you to move your car," The man says again, his tone firmer this time.

"You're blocking traffic." Olivia lets out an almost inscrutable scoff.

"Um, excuse me?" She snaps, and I physically cringe at how uncomfortable it makes me. My sister is so unbelievably blunt, and apparently people of authority are no exception to this rule. "I just told you that we would move. Besides, people can get around us, it's not like there's a line."

"If you don't move your car, I'm going to have no choice but to tow it." Clearly, this person is not pleased with my sister's attitude. She shifts her grip on me, angling herself around so that she can see him better, and I catch a glimpse of the pure resentment in her expression.

"Okay, asshole," Olivia bites out, her determination unfettered by the man's (most likely empty) threats, "My sister is already upset enough, and she hates confrontation. So please, do us both a favor and get lost." I hear the sound of a button being pressed on a radio, and a succession of beeps before the man speaks again.

"Can I get a tow truck to—"

"She said to get lost, asshole!" I cry out, my voice coming out in a squeal. I know that I must look like an insane person based on the look of pure shock that appears on the security guard's features. For someone so bold, he's certainly quite puny, and obviously has never seen a woman who is experiencing heightened emotionality. He looks terrified, and he backs off instantly, tripping over himself as he stumbles away. Olivia shoots me a look, then, and we both burst into laughter. I'm sure that the fact that I'm half laughing, and half weeping makes me seem even more deranged, like one of those hyenas from The Lion King with my disheveled hair and my bloodshot eyes.

"Men will never understand the full range of female emotion. Did you see his face?" Olivia laughs as we start back towards her car, "I mean, he looked like he thought you were going to eat him or something."

"Boil him over my cauldron like a witch, maybe?" I joke, "I mean, I have the hair going for it. I could totally pass as a witch right now."

"I love you so much, and you're so right about that."

"I think it's the eyes, too. This whole 'no sleep' look has to be genuinely terrifying, honestly. I have to give him that."

"That's true. You look scary." As we start to drive away, I let out another laugh. It's half-hearted, but I don't mean for it to be — the lack of sleep and the emotional whiplash are definitely starting to get to me. I feel delirious. Looking out the window of the car, I watch the city appear on the horizon once we pull onto the highway, trees passing in a blur. I have to close my eyes as we speed past all of the signs so that I don't get dizzy.

"I feel bad for whoever that guy's future partner is," I say after a moment, opening one eye to gauge Olivia's reaction. She lets out a small chuckle, nodding in agreement.

"Someone's on a bit of a power trip," Olivia agrees, "You think he's compensating for something?"

"Oh, I'm sure of it. You don't get into a career in airport security unless you're deeply underqualified and deeply overvalue yourself." We laugh again, and for the briefest moment, I feel like everything is normal. But then I see the boarding pass still clutched firmly in my hand and snap back to reality. My laughter fades, and I let my eyes fall closed again, hoping that this will signal for Olivia not to say anything to me. The silence grows between us, but even despite my extreme fatigue, it's fully impossible for me to fall asleep. Between the loud sounds of the road and the bright morning sun streaming in through the windshield and my own racing thoughts, sleep is pretty much hopeless for me.

"We don't have to talk about it, you know," Olivia says, then, breaking me out of my thoughts, "Not until you're ready. But I just..." She pauses and takes a deep breath, and I blink my eyes open, sitting upright to face her. Her eyes are glassy with tears, and she looks like she's trying not to break down. "Whatever it is, you're clearly even more upset than you were the first time you called me about the divorce. And I don't mean that to say that you didn't care about that or anything, I just mean it seems like this is really upsetting you. And I'm here, okay? I'm here."

Her empathy for me is so natural. If I wasn't so exhausted, I would probably start crying again for what feels like the millionth time in the last 24 hours. Instead, I just smile at her, placing my hand on her shoulder briefly.

"I love you. Thank you for coming."

"Please, I never would have just left you to fend for yourself at the airport, that place is horrible." She physically cringes at the thought. "I love you too."

"The rest of it, though, I'm probably going to need to tell you over a bottle of wine."

"Way ahead of you, sis."

***

When we get back to Olivia and Thomas' place, I'm surprised to find a couple of bottles of my favorite rosé on the counter. I want to ask how she got them before I even got here, but she points to Thomas, who's still having coffee on his couch when she walks in. The fact that he was willing to do something like that for me, even though it's a small gesture, makes my heart swell. God, she's really found a good one, I think, giving him a sheepish wave of appreciation as Olivia leads me to their guest bedroom, promptly instructing me to sleep.

And thank God for whoever invented blackout curtains, because I do. Until roughly 4 P.M. that same day.

I'm groggy when I get up and know that I'll probably only be able to last for a few hours until I crash again for the rest of the night. Thomas isn't in the living room or in the kitchen when I walk out, only Olivia, and she's putting away groceries — specifically, two pints of chocolate ice cream.

"You know me so well," I say in lieu of a greeting, and she nods sagely in my direction.

"Pizza is on the way, too. I got us two large cheese pizzas with extra cheese." I almost groan in delight at the thought.

"You're the best big sister ever. You know that, right?"

"You didn't think I was the best big sister ever when I wouldn't let you borrow my prom dress for your Halloween costume—"

"It's probably best for both of us if we don't rehash that specific memory right now." "Fair."

"Thank you for this, though. Seriously," I say as I plop myself down helplessly on the couch, still in the clothes I flew home in. "Honestly, I feel a little bit like a gremlin right now.

Nothing feels real."

"I'll take any excuse I can get for pizza, wine, and ice cream. And you're not a gremlin, I promise, because I fed you after dark before and nothing happened." She pours two (rather large) glasses of wine, then, and walks over to me, sitting crisscross on the couch to face me as she sips hers."

"Okay," I start, "So."

"So."

"I told you about how Beck and I had..." I trail off, trying to find the right words to not sound like a crass teenager. My sister, apparently, cannot be bothered not to, though.

"About how you two fucked?" I actually facepalm and roll my eyes at her.

"Olivia, come on."

"Jeez, okay. Slept together?"

"Yeah, we'll go with that."

"Okay, so. You slept together," Olivia repeats, gesturing in a way that tells me to get to the point, "Then what?"

"Well, there started to be... there started to be feelings."

Olivia doesn't seem to be too surprised by this, so I carry on. I skip over all of the details, glossing over the actual interactions and instead focus on the night that Tristan called me, and how stupid I had made myself look when I picked a fight with Beck over it. Olivia doesn't say much — her face is free of judgment or disappointment. Instead, she takes it all in attentively, sipping her wine occasionally and taking in a deep breath when I get finished telling her what happened.

"Wow," she says, placing her wine glass on a coaster with a little clink, and I rub my temples, still in a mild state of disbelief with myself and the way I acted.

"I know."

"You know that this isn't just about your career questions and the divorce, right?" It's more of a statement than it is a question. She's so matter of fact that it takes me aback for a moment.

"What?"

"The fact that you freaked out on Beck for no reason."

"Okay, well, it definitely wasn't a one-sided argument—"

"I didn't say that. You're scared, Dee." I blink at her rapidly, shaking my head a little.

"I'm sorry? What do you mean?" My voice comes out higher than I intend for it to.

"You started to get feelings for Beck. But your beautiful and gorgeous and deeply intelligent, yet overthinking lawyer brain, got in the way." I pause for a moment, trying to make sense of what she's saying.

"Can you elaborate?"

"You thought, on some level, that it would be easier for you to break things off with Beck on your terms rather than risking losing him again. You thought the pain would be easier to deal with that way. But if I were to venture a guess, it turns out that it's pretty bad anyway, doesn't it?"

Olivia is right. Everything she said is completely correct, right on the nose. But it doesn't mean that I like to hear it. I bury my face in my hands as she speaks, groaning softly once she's done, only somewhat frustrated by the accuracy of her statements.

"Why do you have to know me so well?"

"You're my sister and we're psychically linked," She shrugs, "It's what I do. Also, I've known you for your entire life and I've seen you overthink your way out of buying a t-shirt at a concert. But you rationalize it so well that you disguise your overthinking as logic."

"Wow. Okay."

"Listen, it's gonna be okay. You're going to talk this out with your fancy therapist and figure out what you actually want and what you're doing with your life, and everything will be okay."

"Liv, nobody knows what they're doing with their lives."

"Exactly. So why are you the exception? All we can do is our best every day," Olivia says, and her quiet wisdom in this moment amazes me. "We shouldn't stay up too late, by the way, so you need to pick out a movie for us to watch now."

"What? Why?"

"Because we're flying to Greece tomorrow."

Her words take me by complete surprise. Greece had been the last thing on my mind up until now, somehow, and I know that my face lights up as I nearly jump out of my seat.

"Wait, Greece?" I say, eyes widening, "I thought you couldn't get out of work?" "I can for this. Taking one week off is way easier than taking two weeks off right now.

This is a four-alarm sister emergency, and I need to make sure you still get your dream vacation.

Plus, I paid a lot of money for those tickets and didn't get travel insurance. So, I might as well."

"Hold on," I stop her then, holding up my hands in defense, "You didn't get travel insurance?" She's probably going to think I'm being too serious about this. My point is proven when she rolls her eyes at me, laughing incredulously.

"That entire sentence and the travel insurance is what you latch onto? Typical."

"Oh my God, you always get travel insurance when you're going out of the country.

Everyone knows that. Why didn't you get travel insurance?"

"Is this seriously the point of the conversation we're focusing on? Lydia, I'm taking you to Greece. We're going to go to Acropolis, the Parthenon, all of the ruins, the Temple of Athena that you've always talked about wanting to see—"

"But what about Small & Sparkling?" Olivia waves me off, shrugging like it's not even a big deal.

"Callie is in charge while I'm gone. She's already said she's happy to help. She can handle it."

"You're sure? Is your passport up to date?"

"Oh my God, Lydia, stop overanalyzing this!" She laughs, taking both of my hands in hers earnestly. "It's all taken care of. We're going to Greece, and we are going to have fun, okay?" A long pause passes between us. And then, without warning, I feel a smile start to creep its way onto my face.

"We're going to Greece?"

"We're going to Greece!"

Chapter 20

Beck

As I'm walking through the airport, I can't help but wonder if Lydia is here too.

I don't know what time her flight to Greece is supposed to be or if she's even going. But the airport is one of those liminal spaces where coming and going is the only thing people are there for. An in-between. Everyone is just passing through, and I'm no exception.

When I was here with Lydia before we left for our trip, this place felt full of possibilities. But now, as I see people being reunited and people saying goodbye to each other, I'm filled with nothing but an acute sense of dread.

Then, across the airport, I spot someone who I could swear is Lydia.

Her hair is the same color, in a ponytail the way she always wears it. She's the same height, and even though I can only see the back of her head, she walks the same way, with the same energetic gait. For a moment, I'm frozen. Indecision stops me dead in my tracks, my mind already at war with itself. Should I say something? Should I run after her, chase her down and make her talk to me? Apologize and beg for her forgiveness?

But, she turns her head. It wasn't Lydia I was looking at, but a stranger.

It feels surreal. All of the wishing and the hoping that somehow, maybe it would be her. That beyond all reason, fate would be able to intervene on my behalf, just this once. That I'd finally had the girl of my dreams and lost her in one fell swoop.

I'm shocked out of my train of thought by my phone vibrating in my pocket. I don't really have to guess to know who's calling — it's my sister, and this is the third time she's tried. I know that I need to answer, at least to let her know that I'm at least alive. Once I do, she lets me know that she's already at the airport to pick me up. Of course, I hadn't asked her to, but someone must have told her what was going on, which led her to come to the conclusion that I would need a ride. Word travels fast, I guess.

She takes me straight home, which I'm thankful for. But, she tells me to meet her at a bar tonight for drinks, which I can't really say no to. I could use a beer and a distraction. So, later the same night, I'm there right on time, before Amber even arrives. When she comes sweeping in, I'm only halfway surprised to see that she's dressed almost to the nines. By the local dive bar's standards, that is, which really just means she put in effort when people tended to show up in a come-as-you-are sort of way most of the time.

"Beckster," She says with a grin, hugging me from the side. The childhood nickname usually makes me cringe, but tonight I'm thankful for it. "You look good. Are you okay?"

"I'm here, I guess." Amber slips onto the barstool next to mine, and then I see the door open again out of my peripheral vision. It's Mason and Callie. It doesn't take me long to figure out that Amber is the one behind their arrival, but I still shoot her a glance. I hope it conveys what I'm wondering — Are these people here out of pity or are they here to yell at me for hurting Lydia?

"I invited them," Amber starts, without me having to ask. "Well, I wanted to invite Mason and Thomas be-cause I thought you might need some male friendship at a time like this, but Thomas was already busy, so Mason brought Callie instead. Because, and I quote, 'If we're having a guy's night, she's the closest thing to an-other guy'." She uses air quotes when she says this, and I almost have to laugh at the implication that Thomas would have even come in the first place. Surely he's busy hating me.

"I see." I try my best to smile at Mason and Callie as they walk over, but I'm sure it comes across as pained rather than happy.

"Somebody get this man a beer," Mason says loudly as he crosses over to us, clapping his hand onto my shoulder, "Can't you see he's heartbroken over here?" There aren't any more seats beside us, so Amber goes to ask the hostess for a table while Mason looks at me as though he's known me for far longer than he has.

"Don't worry, man," He continues, "I know you don't have many friends, but I'm not here to judge, just to act as moral support." At this, Callie punches him in the arm. "Ow? What was that for?" I don't know when he came to this conclusion, but he's not too far off. My only real friends are my work friends, since I hardly ever see my college friends anymore.

"Please ignore him," Callie interjects, "He suffered one too many concussions in high school playing soccer. We're sorry about everything that happened, Beck, and we're here for you. I know we've only met each other, like, once, but this is important to Amber, so it's important to us." She seems very genuine, but I can't bring myself to muster anything resembling excitement for this interaction.

"Gee, thanks guys." My voice is flatter than I intended when I say it, but Beck doesn't seem to notice. He swings his arm around my shoulders like we're old friends, leaning across me to try and get someone's attention at the bar.

"Seriously, bartender? What does a man have to do to get his sad..." Mason searches for the word for a moment, "Friend that he's met twice a beer at this establishment?"

Even once we're at the table, I'm still not too enthused by the prospect of the evening at hand. It's a typical Friday night, and there's plenty of people to drown out the (slightly grating) noise of the band that's playing nothing but yacht rock hits. There's a couple who have to be completely wasted who are on the dance floor, dancing to probably the worst rendition of Just the Two of Us that I've ever heard as if they were listening to Pony by Ginuwine instead.

This place isn't one of my usual haunts. It's probably obvious by the look on my face, but once the girls are a couple of drinks in, they join the growing crowd on the dance floor, leaving Mason and I alone at the table as I nurse my Dos Equis. I don't know what compelled him to take pity on me like this for the evening, but I'm almost positive that he would rather be anywhere else. Still, though, he shares some of his opinions on his favorite teams (he speaks very passionately for a solid few minutes about the Philadelphia Eagles and Jason Kelce), and he listens to me intently when I tell him about my interests in pottery and film, specifically Star Wars. He's definitely a lot more "manly" than I am, but he also tells me about his obsession with Lord of the Rings, which I respect deeply. Eventually, of course, the conversation turns to what happened between Lydia and I, and as it turns out, I'm just tipsy enough to where I don't hold back any details. Once I finish telling him everything, he lets out a low whistle, his eyes wide.

"Dude. That's tough." Mason downs the rest of his beer after he says it, crushing the can and pushing it to the edge of the table.

"That's... one way to describe it, yeah." The literal crushing of the beers feeds even further into the frat boy persona that Mason emulates. It's effortless. His happy-go-lucky attitude is exactly what I would expect from someone with, apparently, a long history of head injuries.

"I mean, I can't imagine how it must feel. Finally getting what you want after all those years only to have it blow up in your face like that." My brow furrows.

"I don't know if that's—"

"Dude, it blew up in your face." Mason gestures in what I assume to be an approximation of an explosion as he says this. As though to give me a visual. I've heard the term 'himbo' thrown around before in certain circles, and I think, then, that if you were to look up the dictionary definition of the word, there would be a photo of Mason next to it. "That's not your fault, I don't think it's anything you did. Clearly, she's just got some stuff to work on. And maybe you do too, I don't know. But you can't let this be the thing that keeps you from ever trying again."

For a moment, I sit in contemplative silence. It's actually good advice, which surprises me, considering the concussions. I nod at him gratefully and a grin breaks out across his features.

"Okay, yeah," I say, "Thanks."

"Don't mention it," Mason responds with a shrug, and we fall into silence again. As I finish the last of my beer, I follow Mason's eyes as they drift away from our table and toward the dance floor. Toward Callie. The way he looks at her, the mix of pride and affection and sadness in his eyes — it's all too familiar. I know that I used to, and probably still do, look at Lydia that way. His advice being so sound makes a lot more sense now. I wonder, then, if the scheme to get the two of them together is really so baseless, after all, or if it's rooted in something more.

"Don't take this the wrong way," I start, Mason's attention finally steering back towards me, "But you seem to know a lot about wanting things that you can't have." I tilt my head in Callie's direction, and he follows with his gaze; When he sees Callie and he understands what I'm implying, his entire face colors a bright shade of red.

"What?" He exclaimed, "Dude, are you kidding?" Mason starts to laugh, then, but it's very forced, the discomfort in his eyes giving him away. "It's Callie. I mean, I just— It's Callie."

"Saying that over and over again doesn't erase the fact that you haven't stopped staring at her for the last ten minutes. Or that you seem to go with her wherever she asks." I'm really not trying to pry or push him to tell me things that he's uncomfortable saying out loud. But, when he looks at her again, I can tell that it's hopeless. He's in love with her, and probably has been for quite some time. Mason's quiet, for a while. But as the waitress brings us another round of beers, he deflates and cracks his open with a long sigh, slumping down in the booth.

"I don't know, man. I just..." Mason takes a breath, steeling himself. "I know it probably doesn't seem different for me and Callie, but it is. We haven't been friends for nearly as long as you guys have, for sure, but I would venture a guess that you never really put yourself out there to Lydia, did you?" At this, I shake my head.

"Right. Well, I did," Mason continues, "And it didn't go well. Asked her to prom in front of all of our friends and she just stood there staring at me while the rest of our friends laughed. I think they thought it was a prank, and she just didn't say anything, so I had to go along with the whole prank thing. We didn't talk to each other for nearly a full month after that. Until that asshole Jacob Thompson stood her up for prom and I went with her anyway. We didn't match, but we ended up forming a truce that night, I think. At least in my mind. We pretty much just went on like nothing happened." He takes a long swig of his beer, then, his attention drifting back over to where Callie is dancing. "I don't know. We were kids. We never really talked about it again after that."

"You do know that she could have wanted to say yes, right?" I ask him, leaning forward, "But was deterred by all of your friends? Thought that they might have been laughing at her too?" Suddenly, his expression looks as though he's in serious thought.

"You know, I never really thought about that." He doesn't get the chance to continue that thought, because as soon as he says it, Callie and Amber make their way back to the booth for a break and some water. Mason falls silent quickly, and I follow suit, but Callie raises her eyebrows, her eyes darting back and forth between the two of us.

"Woah, you guys got quiet fast," She quips, laughing softly and scooting into the booth next to Mason, "Were you talking about us?" Mason looks aghast at this question.

"Pfft. What? No." He tries to wave her off and act nonchalant, but his voice is far too loud and exaggerated, his dishonesty obvious.

"Okay, liar," Callie retorts, folding her arms across her chest. Mason mirrors her posture, as if he's a 10-year-old mocking a girl on the playground.

"I'm rubber and you're glue."

"Well, that's obviously not true, because I made a statement. How could I be the one that's a liar? It's not logical, Mase."

"Doesn't matter. I'm rubber and you're glue." Callie rolls her eyes, and for a moment, I think I'm looking at a mirror image of how Lydia and I used to act around each other. Before Heather. Before Tristan. Amber must see it, too, because she's quick to change the subject.

"Have you guys been doing some bonding?" She asks me.

"No," I say, tone dripping with sarcasm, "We've actually just been sitting here looking at each other and not talking."

"Oh. That's super weird, you guys. Why are you doing that?"

"Endurance challenge," Mason says, and he raises his beer towards me.

"First one to break and talk loses," I agree with a laugh.

"Wait, that doesn't make any sense," Callie starts, eyes narrowing, "Because wouldn't you have just lost, Beck?"

"No," I reply, "Because it's not about either of our personal lives or feelings." Callie scoffs at this.

"You guys are so weird."

"But that's what makes us fun," Mason retorts, letting his arm rest across the back of the booth around her shoulders, "Sorry we can't all be squares."

"Oh my God, who says squares?" She leans into him, and I wonder if she even notices she's doing it. "What are you, a villainous oil barron from the 1930's?"

"No, I'm hotter than all those guys. Have you seen pictures of all of them? They're all ugly."

"We are so off topic right now," Amber says, interrupting their train of thought, "What are we even talking about? This is supposed to be about Beck."

"Oh, I don't think I want this to be about me." Shaking my head, I take another sip of my beer, willing it to dull my senses. I've never liked attention. Today is no exception to that rule. "I can't handle another emotional conversation. If anything, I need a distraction."

"But—"

"Oh, come on, let the man have some fun." Mason flags down our waitress after he effectively silences

Amber. "Excuse me, ma'am, can we get another round over here?"

"And a round of tequila shots," I add, much to Amber's obvious disgust.

"What?"

"It's supposed to be about me, right?" Amber doesn't look pleased with me. I don't blame her — the alcohol has started to go to my head and is definitely doing its job, numbing all of my emotions. Stripping me of any sense of self-consciousness and allowing me to focus fully on my blatant self-pity instead. I know I'll regret it tomorrow. I know drinking doesn't ever really make you forget.

But it can dull the pain of losing the one woman I've always loved, at least temporarily.

Chapter 21

Lydia

Greece is absolutely everything that I imagined and more.

And by that, I mean that it feels like I stepped right into Mamma Mia.

The beaches and the people and the foliage are all so colorful and bright and full of life. History surrounds me at every corner in Athens, and cobblestone pathways and dirt roads wind through beautiful classical architecture on the islands. I'm surrounded by the sweetest cats everywhere we go, too, which is an added bonus. One of the cats that comes up to us at a café that we visit is the sweetest little tabby girl, and for a moment, I try to talk Olivia into taking her home with us. She talks me down, though, when she mentions the struggle of trying to get said cat through customs, and that if she stays here, she'll be loved by even more people who get to meet her.

I cry when we leave the café.

Just like all good things, though, our week in paradise comes to an end far too soon. I'd love to be able to say that I didn't think about Beck at all, but that wouldn't be true. I found him around every corner, down every road, imagining what it would have been like if he had been there with me instead.

Once we're home again, and I'm trying to make my way back into my reality of meetings and case briefings, I sink fully into the regret of it all. I miss Beck. I miss him terribly, and I realize without a doubt that I'm the one that's in the wrong. That I'm the one that messed it up.

Worst of all, I realize that I'm in love with him. Completely, terribly, and hopelessly in love with him.

Going back to work is strange. Almost like an out-of-body experience. I know it's only been a few weeks by the time I'm there, but it takes me nearly a full month to adjust to being back. Even then, I don't know if I can call it adjusting, because before, all I wanted to do while I was at work was to give my clients the best results possible. To learn and to grow and to study as much of how the law works as possible.

But now, I know what else is out there. Now, I'm longing for my days at the beach, for the simple joys of writing and being with Beck. Now, I try not to think about how it's been a little over a month since Beck and I have even spoken. And now, I'm lucky if I'm able not to fall asleep during the numerous Zoom calls.

It's during one of these aforementioned Zoom calls, about a month after we got home from Greece, where I'm jolted out of my trance by a phone call from my sister. I don't even know what the meeting I'm in is about, if I'm honest, so I don't feel bad about it when I decide to answer. I make sure that my end of the call is muted, and I pick up the phone.

"Hello?"

"Okay, Lydia," My sister's voice chirps through the speaker, louder than I expected. I have to pull my phone away from my ear to turn the volume down. "You have to promise me you're not going to get mad when I tell you this."

"That's never a good way to start a conversation," I say bluntly, kicking my feet up onto my desk.

"I'm serious," Olivia continues, and my brow furrows. "I'm trying to do something helpful, something that's going to be beneficial to you. So, you have to promise me that you're not going to be angry."

"I can't promise that?" I try to keep my voice level, even though I have a sneaking suspicion that this is going to become one of those moments where my sister irritates me far more than any human ever thought possible. "How can I promise that when I don't even know what it is?" There's silence and the sound of a copier buzzing in the background. Olivia sighs before she speaks again.

"Okay," She starts, and I hear the click of heels on the hard floor. She's pacing in her office, which means she's clearly nervous about whatever it is she's going to tell me. "You remember how we were talking about the journals you wrote about Greece? The part about the

Temple of Athena in particular?" The conversation we had a few weeks ago comes to mind. I'd shown Olivia the night that I wrote it, and she'd been pestering me about submitting it for publication ever since. I know what she's going to say before she even says it. "And about the friend that I have who works in the travel publishing industry?" I stand, then, palm pressed firmly against my forehead in frustration as I audibly groan.

"Liv, you didn't."

"I didn't even ask him to publish it!" My sister insists, "Just to read it, I promise!" Even the thought of someone who I don't fully trust reading the words I'd written just for myself threatens to make me break out in hives.

"Oh my God. Olivia, you know how self-conscious I get about this stuff, I mean—"

"Lydia, he thought it was amazing."

I'm stunned into silence. I don't think that I ever even imagined that this would be the case. That someone who doesn't know me with some actual agency in a creative industry would find my words useful. Would enjoy what I had to say. I've always told myself they were childish.

Superficial. Unimportant. I know I'm my own worst critic, but there are so many people out there with so much experience, I just thought there would be no way I could ever compete. I don't know how long I'm quiet for, but it's obviously long enough for Olivia to think she dropped the call, because her words coming over the speaker are the only thing that makes me remember I'm actively having a conversation.

"Hello?" I hear her ask, with an insistent tone to her voice, "Dee, you there?" "I'm here."

"So, say something!"

"I'm mad that you did this without telling me," I say truthfully, staring out my office window and rubbing one of my temples with my free hand.

"Well, I'm telling you now—"

"Doesn't count. I still get to be angry about that part." I can tell that she knows I'm right, because she lets out a huff, and I hear her heels stop clicking.

"Okay, I guess that's fair."

"But" I start, and she sighs again. I know she thinks she knows where I'm going with this. Regardless, I press on. "You did something for me that I wouldn't have had the guts to do for myself. I know that. So, thank you."

"Oh." For once, Olivia is the one who's left speechless. "Really?"

"Yes, Olivia. Thank you."

"I'd do anything for you, Dee," she says, conviction and sincerity clear in her voice.

"And, just so we're clear, I definitely would also do it again without your permission."

"I know," I laugh, shaking my head incredulously. Sure, I've always been the romantic, but my sister, on the other hand, has always been the practical go-getter. I get so worked up in my own fears sometimes that I can't act on things that matter, even if deep down, I know I really want them. "So, I mean," I continue, moving to sit back down at my desk, "He really liked it? He wasn't just saying it out of pity or because he knows that I'm your sister?"

"I actually didn't tell him you were my sister. I just said I had someone who'd written an amazing travel piece that unfortunately wouldn't be a fit for Small & Sparkling and left out your name. I only had to give it to him when he decided to publish it."

Emotional whiplash. Again, I'm in disbelief, sitting on the edge of my seat and blinking rapidly.

"Wait, what?" I only had to give it to him when he decided to publish it. Not if he decided to publish it, but when he decided to.

"I said he didn't only like the story because it was yours, since he didn't know who had written it—"

"No, not that part."

"Oh. I didn't mean anything bad about it by not publishing it to Small & Sparkling."

"The part when you said that he'd... already decided to publish it?"

"Oh!" Olivia cheers, clapping her hands together excitedly. "Yes! Your story is coming out in next month's publication! Isn't that great?"

"No!"

"What?" She asks, clearly as shocked as I am by the bluntness of my refusal. "What do you mean no?"

"I mean no, Olivia. I mean that you shouldn't have done this without asking my permission first. I'm pretty sure it's illegal."

"Well, actually, it's not illegal, because you consented." I let out a frustrated groan at this. Not only is my sister going behind my back, but she's bringing legal issues into the things she's doing behind my back, too.

"You forged my consent?"

"Maybe a little."

"Now, that's definitely illegal—"

"Okay, God, I get it. You went to law school."

"This is serious, Liv!" I insist, trying to convey the severity. "What if my firm gets wind of this? What if they read it and they... I don't know, they decide that it's not a good look for the firm? They don't want me pursuing side jobs?"

"They don't own you," Olivia says simply. I can almost picture the shrug she pairs with her nonchalant words. "Plus, if it somehow makes them look bad that one of their junior partners is a super talented writer and a hottie who loves to travel, then that's on them."

"Hottie? Wait, did you submit a picture?"

"I had to! For the article! It's flattering, it's one of the ones you said was good." At this, I groan for probably the tenth time in this conversation.

"What if they think it's unprofessional?"

"Then they can take it up with you. I, personally would think it's really dumb for them not to let you, you know, do what you want with your free time?"

"There are corporate policies—"

"Oh, screw the corporate policies!" This time, it's her turn to be firm with me. It knocks me off kilter for a moment. "You don't even want to work there anymore anyways, Dee."

"When did I say that? I didn't say that."

"You didn't have to. I know you, remember?"

I hate the fact that she's right. Honestly, I don't know how to admit to myself that I'm excited about this prospect, much less to her. Not when I know she'll get some weird satisfaction out of being right, like she always used to when we were younger. But, God, I am excited. It all hits me at once, that familiar feeling in the pit of my stomach, the butterflies and the flips and all of the jitters.

"I know," I say to her, finally, my smile evident in my voice.

"So, you forgive me?"

"I didn't say that."

"But you will eventually, right?"

"I forgave you after you stole my Polly Pocket lunchbox, so I guess I can't ever really stay that mad at you."

When we get off the phone, I have another meeting with another team of partners. Instead of sadness, though, I'm distracted by possibility, by the thrill of something new.

This could be it. The thing I've been looking for. And I'm hoping so desperately that it is.

Chapter 22

Lydia

Two Months Later

I watch with bated breath as the comments on my article tick up and up and up. Practical Travel has been the go-to for normal people going on a normal, reasonably priced vacation since its first publication 12 years ago, and now, my words are part of that legacy. I almost don't know how to reconcile it.

No, I definitely don't know how to reconcile it.

The comments hit fifty. Then they hit seventy-five. I have to force myself to stop looking around eleven P.M., when they hit two hundred.

When I wake up, there are nearly one thousand comments. I almost throw my phone across my bedroom in shock. So, I run out of the room instead, to find Amber and Melanie enjoying an otherwise peaceful morning. I must look terrifying, because as soon as I burst through the door, both of them jump, and Amber spills her coffee on the counter.

"God! I'm so sorry!"

"No, it's fine, at least it wasn't on me — is everything okay?" She furrows her eyebrows, a look of deep concern etched across her features. "You look like you got struck by lightning or something."

"Yeah, everything is fine!" I didn't look in the mirror before I sprinted out into the living room, so I can only assume that I look like a swamp creature or something of the sort. My hair is always crazy in the mornings before I brush it, so I'm sure it looks like a rat's nest up there. "It's my article! People actually like it!"

"Hey, that's awesome!" Amber cheers, clasping her hands together. Melanie's excitement is more subdued but present all the same.

"Good!" Melanie says, beaming. "We told you it would be a hit."

"We did, didn't we?" Amber laughs, standing up to hug me. When she pulls away, she keeps her hands planted squarely on my shoulders, looking me in the eye intensely. "For the record, I never doubted you for a second. I kind of feel like a proud parent, though, which is fun."

"I don't know what I'm supposed to do about it, though," I say, pushing a hand through my mess of hair. "The writing, I mean. And all of the comments."

"Are there a lot?" Amber asks.

"1,800, last I checked." She lets out a low whistle of amazement, and for a moment, reminds me so much of her brother that I think I could cry.

"Wow, okay, that is a lot. Don't people usually say not to read those things? Like, I've heard all those famous people talk about how terrible it is to google themselves, or about terrible things they've read in comments sections."

"I know!" I probably sound a little too exasperated, particularly for someone who's had a dream of theirs come true practically overnight. Still, though, I cross over to the couch, slumping down in a heap and staring at the ceiling. "I want to read them, mostly for feedback purposes, but I don't know what to do."

"Do you want one of us to look first?" Melanie asks, "To tell you if you should avoid the comment section?"

"Yes. Wait— no. I don't know." I say, my insecurities threatening to run rampant. My indecisiveness is fueled by an acute sense of dread that I'm not good enough, that I'm an imposter, that no one cares to hear what I have to say. I know that I'm my own worst critic, that what they are going to say really can't be that bad, but my imagination is already running wild with all of the possibilities. "If you tell me to avoid it, I'm just going to be sad and read the whole thing out of self-loathing."

"That's a good point," Melanie adds, and I groan, leaning forward and propping my elbows onto my knees, burying my face into my hands.

"Okay. Maybe I should just flip a coin? I don't know. I'm just so—" My train of thought is interrupted by my phone ringing in my pocket. I have no idea who would be calling me this early, other than my sister or my mom. But, when I read the name that appears on the screen, I freeze.

Jake Sanchez, the Editor in Chief of Practical Travel is calling me.

"Oh," I start, feeling the all too familiar panic starting to rise in my chest. "Oh my God. I have to take this."

"What? Who is it?" Amber asks, jumping up out of her seat, her eyes wide and full of hope. "Is it Beck?" At that, I shoot her a look.

"Sorry. Just... kind of hoped."

"It's Jake. From the magazine. "

"Oh my God, you have to take that!" Amber echoes me, waving her hands at me as if to tell me to hurry up and do it already. "Answer!"

"Hello?" I try desperately to ignore the fact that I can hear my heartbeat in my own ears as I answer the call.

"Hey there, Lydia!" Jake says, sounding cheerful. Hopefully that's a good sign, but then again, every time that we've had a conversation, he sounds cheerful. So, it could mean nothing.

"How's it going?"

"I'm okay, I think?" I say, wincing at myself. A bit too honest, probably.

"You think?"

"Yeah, I just—" I start, and then I sigh, trying hard to resist the urge to bite my fingernails down to the quick. My leg bounces involuntarily. "It's all a little overwhelming. I don't really know what to do with all of it. Where to start."

"You haven't looked at the comment section yet, have you?"

I'm silent for a beat. I don't know what prompted him to ask, but of course, my initial instinct is to automatically assume the worst-case scenario. That the article bombed so horrifically that they're going to pull it from publication. Or that somehow, my article caused someone to die in a horrible manner. That someone had been reading it on their way to work and hated it so much that it caused them to walk into traffic or something and that I'm now going to get sued. My mind is moving too rapidly for me to keep up. The possibilities for the ways that my dream could end before it's even really gotten started seem endless.

"No?" I say finally, trying to ward off the shake in my voice. My anxiety is palpable, a tangible thing that won't leave me alone. "Should I? I mean, there's so many of them, and I don't really know what to—"

"They love you, Lydia," Jake cuts me off, his tone changing from unreasonably chipper to gentle reassurance. "The readers." I blink rapidly and sit up straight, unsure how to process what it is that I've just heard.

"What?"

"I haven't seen this many positive comments that are specifically about the way an article makes them feel. About how it really sends them into the world the writer is trying to create, about how engaging it is to read. You're a hit, Lydia."

"You're kidding."

"I'm not."

"No, you have to be messing with me," I insist, standing to run a shaking hand through my hair as I pace around the living room. It's difficult to ignore Amber and Melanie's expectant glances, but I try anyway, keeping my eyes locked firmly on my feet. "This has to be a prank. I'm getting punked."

"Here," Jake starts, clearing his throat, "'Whoever wrote this deserves a raise. Not only is it informative, but it's also deeply moving. The author's quick wit and relatability made it seem like there isn't anything being in Greece can't cure, even a broken heart.'"

"Oh." I'm unable to think, unable to form a sentence that would even begin to express how unreasonably seen that this analysis makes me feel. I can't believe that someone would actually think that about the silly things that I wrote in my journal, about the escape from reality that I had needed to manufacture for myself to feel like a human again after what happened between Beck and me. It's overwhelming, threatening to topple me like a wave. "Wow."

"There's more. 'I've never wanted to get broken up with so badly just so I could travel to Greece and experience it exactly this way. There's so much emotion in the way the writer describes the people, the architecture, the must-visit spots, it's almost like reading a romance novel.'"

"And you're not making this up?" I ask him again, in complete disbelief. The compliments, while deeply encouraging, also teeter on becoming... overwhelming.

"Not a word of it," Jake assures me.

"Okay."

"Do you need to hear more?"

"No, I don't think I can," I answer honestly. I've never been good at accepting praise, at receiving compliments. This is no exception to that rule. In fact, it's the opposite; Even though I'm obviously glad that the comments aren't negative, the weight of expectation that I feel I'll need to live up to is crushing.

"That's fine. But just so you know, I'm calling because we would love it if you would come on with us full-time."

If I wasn't overwhelmed before, I am now. Not only do the readers enjoy what I have to say, but the publishers do too. So much so that they want me to do this, and only this for a living. Travel. My one true passion. Never in my wildest dreams did I think something like this could happen. My anxiety has shifted sources — I'm no longer feeling threatened by the possibility of criticism, but by the possibility of change. Major change, in fact. I let myself feel this for a moment, trying my best to acknowledge it and name it, the way that my therapist has taught me. My anxiety takes many forms, so I've been working on naming it, particularly after realizing that fear of change was the real root of what went wrong between Beck and I. Gradually, my breathing starts to slow, and I remind myself that I'm the one who's in control of my body. I know that I've probably been quiet for far too long when Jake's voice finally comes across the line again.

"Lydia? Are you there?" He asks, breaking the silence.

"I'm here," I say, willing myself to sound confident and not like I'm spiraling.

"You don't have to decide now," Jake replies, as though he can sense how conflicted I am based purely on my tone. "Take your time. I know that this isn't an easy decision to make. But, at the very least, if you decide not to change careers, we would love to get any submissions from you. Even if they're only on a periodic basis."

"Really?" For some reason, this shocks me, too. The fact that they want to publish more of my work so badly that they'd accept part-time submissions from me instead feels foreign to me.

"Yes. You're good at this, and you have a clear passion for it. You can see it in the quality of your work. Just think about it, okay?"

"Alright," I nod, even though I know he can't see what I'm doing. "Okay. Thank you, Jake."

"Talk to you soon."

After he hangs up the phone, the gears are already turning. It would be so huge to make a career change like this, particularly with everything else that's already going on in my life. I'm supposed to be closing on the house in a month. My boss and I are setting ourselves up to take on our biggest case yet. I'm already touring new houses and getting ready to move for the second time in a year. Whether or not I can really handle a career change on top of all of that, too, is out of the question. But, if Practical Travel is willing to take my submissions, maybe I can start out on a more part-time basis. See if it's something that I can see myself doing long-term, test the waters.

I'm also hesitant to jump in because I'm still reeling from all of the change that took place in just a span of a few weeks before the vacation. The divorce was finalized, I had Beck, and I lost him again, and I'm the one to blame for that. Trying to handle more change right now would be like an unstoppable force and an immovable object. Frankly, impossible.

I've already started over once this year. I don't know if I have it in me to start over again.

"So?" Amber says after a long while, snapping me out of my train of thought. I'd been staring out the window with my phone still pressed to my ear, and I jump slightly when I hear her voice, having forgotten that there were other people in the room with me. When I turn to face them, they're both looking at me intently, waiting for me to say something. I take a deep breath, and then I answer.

"He wants me to write full-time."

Amber squeals with excitement when I say this, and I break out into a wide smile that I had no idea I would be

able to muster. She runs over, hugging me, Melanie joining her. For a moment, I feel as elated as they do. Filled
with possibility and hope and expectation for what feels
like the first time in a long time. As they're congratulating me, though, my mind interrupts the celebration with
a realization that rocks me to my core.

I'm celebrating my accomplishments with the wrong
Shepherd.

My cheeks are wet with tears before I even realize
that I'm crying. Sadness and regret wash over me like a
tide, all because I know that I should have been sharing
a moment like this with Beck. And that I'm the one to
blame for messing it all up in the first place.

"Woah, Lydia, hey," Amber says gently, pulling away
from the hug and placing her hands on my shoulders,
concern etched across her features. "What's wrong?"

"Nothing. Everything. I don't know," I say, trying and
failing to put into words the emotional rollercoaster that
I've been on in the past few minutes. People like my
writing. So much so that they want to pay me to travel.
But my life has changed so much, I don't know how to
reconcile it all or even how to begin putting it into words.
And I know that I lost my chance at a happy ending,
that it's all my fault. Suddenly, I find myself laughing
through the tears at the insanity of it all. "They're kind
of happy tears? But they're not? I'm conflicted and sad
and excited and overwhelmed and I miss Beck and—"

"You miss him?" Amber's face lights up, as though
she's just been given the best news of her life. She's

obviously excited by the revelation, but I only find myself crying even harder. Now that it's out there, now that I've named it and called attention to it, it's all that I can think about. I miss Beck. I miss him terribly and have no idea how to fix what I've broken.

"I miss him so much," I say through broken sobs, my shoulders (and my entire body) shaking. Amber, to my surprise, lets out a sigh of relief, pulling me into a tight hug.

"Thank God," She says, "I've been waiting for you to say that."

"What?" My voice is thick with tears, and I wipe my eyes with the back of my sleeve.

"You have?"

"Of course I have. Lydia, he's crazy about you. He made me promise not to say anything unless you did, but he's been miserable for months." Her words hit me like a blow to the chest.

"Have you just been talking to both of us behind our backs and waiting for me to say something?" I had, of course, given Amber my side of the story on what happened on the trip.

Nothing too detailed, but enough to let her know that Tristan had really gotten into my head. That I probably wasn't ready for whatever was going on with Beck based on how unsteady I felt once I actually considered how everything happened. I'd also told her about the conversations I'd been having with my therapist, naturally, because that's the kind of thing you do with your best friends. Overshare.

"Obviously I've been talking to both of you about it," Amber tells me, like it's beyond question. Which, to her credit, it kind of is. "He's my brother and you're my roommate. Not exactly an avoidable topic."

"So... what do I do? I don't know if I can just... talk to him after all this, I treated him so unfairly—"

"That's true, but you were also being manipulated by your ex-husband to think the way you did. I promise, I know my brother. He'll understand. Besides, he's crazy about you anyway, so even if it weren't perfectly logical, he would probably still forgive you."

"I was out of that relationship for a long time before it ever actually ended," I say plainly, and Amber and Lydia both smile softly at me.

"I know that, Dee," Amber nods, pulling me in for another hug. I accept it gratefully, pulling Melanie into the hug with us.

"This still doesn't fix the whole 'I have no idea what to do' thing," I say after a moment.

"You don't have to do anything." Amber grins as she looks at me, and I furrow my brow at the mischievous look on her face.

"Wait, what? What do you mean? I need to talk to him, I don't—"

"You can talk to him at his house tonight."

"How do you even know he'll be there?" I ask, feeling my nerves starting to creep up again. God, I hope I don't break out in hives. "I should say something to him beforehand—"

"He'll be there." She sounds certain when she says this. "Tell him you want to talk, tell him you're coming over, then don't say anything else once he's read the message." It's like she has this completely thought out. Honestly, I kind of marvel at the ingenuity of it. This way, I don't have to panic over whether or not he's going to text me back the whole time.

My heart is pounding. My mind is racing. I'm going to see Beck again tonight, and all I can do is hope that he gives me another chance.

Chapter 23

Beck

After the vacation, all of the days started to bleed into one another. The only bright spots were the days I had my pottery classes. When I was at the wheel, I forgot everything else for a while. Forgot myself, forgot how pointless work seemed, forgot how I'd come so close to being with the love of my life only to have her slip right out of my reach.

But when the wheel stopped turning, my mind pursued me relentlessly with thoughts of her.

Lydia was in my dreams. She was on crowded streets, in coffee shops, even in my office at times. Of course, it was never actually her, which only made me miss her even more. A cruel twist of fate. I knew, deep down, that the only reason I thought I was seeing her as often as I did was because I wanted to see her so badly. My mind was playing tricks on me, and my heart was the one to blame for it.

It's on one of the days that's the same as all of the others that it happens. I'm at work, staring mindlessly at my laptop, pretending to be working on a task that's really just an empty Word document. Then, I feel my phone buzz twice in my pocket.

When I see the text from my sister, I close my work laptop immediately.

From: Amber (sis)
BECK
BECK, IT'S HAPPENING, SHE MISSES YOU
I TOLD YOU SO

My first reaction is to assume that Amber is pulling a (very mean) prank on me. She's usually not the type to do something like that, so for a moment, I'm angry that she would choose this topic, this moment to start doing so. Amber knows well enough how horrible these past couple of months have been for me. For her to make light of it now is just cruel, and I've got half a mind to start to tell her so.

As I'm typing my response, though, I see another notification come up across my screen, and I freeze.

From: Lydia M.
Hi. I've been an idiot. I'm coming over tonight so we can talk. Hope that's okay. Be there around 7.

For a second, I consider the very real possibility that my brain has stopped working. Short-circuited... A colleague passes by my office, and out of the corner of my eye, I notice him trying to wave at me. But I don't respond. I can't. I'm staring off into space, and all I can think about is how I have no idea what to expect. I've wanted this for months, have been holding out hope for this to happen, but I don't think I ever fully expected it to.

Should I respond? Should I text Amber first? Should I just go home now and wait until she gets there? God, what if Amber's wrong and she just misses being my friend? If I wasn't already hopeless for the rest of the workday, I am now. It doesn't take me long at all to consider the merits of taking a half day. I have so much unused vacation time from the past few years that it's practically coming out of my ears. And besides, I'm not being useful anyways, so without hesitation, I send a quick email to my boss. Within five minutes, I'm out the door, my mind already spinning relentlessly with ideas for what to do and what to say when I finally text Amber.

Amber (sis):Okay. Wow.
Beck: [. . .]
Beck: Well, I guess you can say 'I told you so.'
Amber: GOOD
Amber: BECAUSE I LITERALLY DID TELL YOU SO
Beck: Alright, don't gloat.
Beck: I need your help with something.

***

By the time 7:00 rolls around, I've lost all concept of time. The afternoon had gone by so slowly and so quickly at the same time that my concept of reality had become somewhat warped. I was so busy trying to get ready to see Lydia again, cleaning my house and preparing everything that the entirety of the afternoon felt like it was in fast forward.

I was completely ready around 5:30, though, and have been sitting on my couch and waiting ever since; It's been the longest hour and a half of my life. Watching the seconds tick by on my clock, the hyperawareness that I have of Lydia's impending arrival makes it seem to move slower and slower and slower.

And then, just as I'm about to get up and start pacing the living room for what feels like the hundredth time that day, there's a knock on the door.

My heart jumps. I take a deep breath, trying to steady myself, but I'm more nervous now than I was when it had been three years since I'd seen her. So much has changed since then between us, and I don't know how to reconcile it all. No amount of planning, no amount of preparation could ever fully ease my nerves, though, and I know that.

It's a leap of faith. Everything is. And no matter how unprepared I think I am, there's nothing I can do or could have ever done to make myself fully ready. I just have to trust and let myself fall.

I open the door and finally lay eyes on her for the first time in months, and my heart is lodged in my throat. She's so beautiful, I can hardly think.

"Lydia," I say simply, and her eyes widen as she looks past me and into my living room, covering her mouth in shock.

"Oh my God, Beck."

Rows upon rows of flowers line the perimeter of my living room. I have at least 14 large planters of African violets that I picked out especially for her, her favorite. There's a candlelit pathway through the foyer (Amber's idea), making the walkway look more like an aisle than a narrow hall. Naturally, though, all of this wasn't going to be enough to fill up an entire room — so the rest of the space is decorated with countless other bouquets of flowers, most of them purple. I even managed to find some wisteria and baby's breath to drape from my mantle, giving the entire living room the look of a greenhouse or a garden. It looks like something out of a fairytale.

I don't know what I expected Lydia's reaction to be to all of it, but once I turn around to face her again after showing her inside, the shocked expression on her face is... unreadable. I'm unable to discern whether it's a good reaction or a bad one, and so immediately, I panic. I've done too much, made too much of a scene out of what should be a simple reunion. My heart rate picks up again and I quickly step in front of her, taking both of her hands in mine.

"Okay, the flowers were probably a lot, I can see that now," I start, my mouth moving faster than my brain. "God, it looks like The Great Gatsby in here. I swear I'm not a psychopath.

If you hate the flowers, it's not going to hurt my feelings, I'll donate them to a funeral home or something—"

"Don't send my flowers to a funeral home!" Lydia cries out, her eyes finally snapping back to mine, where before they'd been fixed on the display.

"Oh," I manage lamely, swallowing down my fear.

"I love them," She continues, looking at me earnestly and squeezing my hands. "I love it. This is..." I can tell that she needs a moment to process it all, because she takes in a deep breath, her eyes glassy with emotion. As she continues, she steps towards me again, her smile growing wider than it was before. I smile back softly, feeling my anxiety start to ease. "It's perfect. You are perfect."

As I stand there with Lydia's hands in mine, I am deeply certain of one thing; I love her, and I'll do anything she asks, so long as she gives me another chance.

"I know you came here because you wanted to talk," I start, letting my thumbs rub comforting circles against the backs of her hands. "And I didn't do this to try and get out of that. I want you to say everything you need to say. I want us to say everything that we need to say to get this behind us. This is just my way of showing you...

of showing you how much I care. So, I guess I'll start."
Lydia nods at me slowly, supportively, giving me the reassurance that I need to continue.

"I am so, so unbelievably sorry for the things I said to
you when we fought." There's a slight shake to my voice,
but I press on. "There's nothing that I can do or say to
take it back, and I've regretted it every day since the
end of the trip. You were going through something, and
I treated it as a personal attack, when it wasn't about me
at all. I let my insecurities get in the way. I can see that
now, and I'm sorry. But Lydia, you have to know," As I'm
starting to tear up, I notice that she is, too. If I wasn't already going to be a mess before, I'll be one now. "I meant
the other things I said. Every single word."

"I love you so much. I've loved you since we were
kids. I've always hoped someday you'd love me back.
Held onto that hope like a life preserver on the ocean
for a long, long time. Your friendship saved me when we
were kids. You make me laugh; you make me remember
what it means to be human. After Heather, I didn't think
that was possible." Before I can continue, I have to wipe
my eyes, the tears clouding my vision. Gently, I swipe
Lydia's away too where they've started to fall, my thumb
gently trailing across her cheekbone as I cup her face in
my hand.

"I love you, Lydia Michaelson. I always have. And it's
about damn time I got the nerve to tell you. To do something about it. I'm tired of... I'm tired of just letting life
happen to me. I want to make my own way. I want to live

a life I care about. And I care about you. I understand if this is too much. I understand if you want to take it slow, to start over. But I can't keep... Can't keep not telling you how I feel. That's what got us into this mess in the first place. So, I love you. And that isn't going to change."

For a moment, she observes me, her bottom lip quivering. She leans her face into my touch, though, and when she smiles at me, my heart soars.

"It took both of us to cause that fight at the beach, Beck. It wasn't just you. Not by a long shot," Lydia starts with a careful laugh, her free hand moving to mirror mine as she holds the side of my face. "I mean, it actually took just me to start it, but it also took me to choose to take my anger out on you instead of dealing with it like an adult. I had so many feelings that were all so intense, I had no idea how to name them. Or where to put them. And so, I just... erupted." Her eyes downcast, she takes a moment, steeling herself with a shaky breath.

"So, I'm sorry, too. And I've been in a lot of therapy, trying to sort it out. Putting names to the things that I've been feeling. I mean, God, you wouldn't believe the things I've had to tell my therapist these past few months. She's gotten an earful." Lydia laughs in spite of herself, and I can't help but smile — her sense of humor and mine have always been the same. "Sorry. I'm getting off topic. Anyway, what I realized... What I realized is that what I was feeling the most was afraid. Afraid of feeling things too deeply. Afraid of getting hurt. Afraid of messing it up and losing you again. And look how that last one turned out." We laugh again, and she shakes her head as she does so, clearly trying to find the right words to convey what it is that she needs to.

"Okay, uh, self-deprecating humor isn't cute. I'm done with that. God. I've been so scared to admit this to my-self, even. I'm so nervous right now that I feel like I'm going to explode. But Beck, oh my God, I love you. I wish I could say that I always knew, but I didn't — not until looking back on my life without rose-colored glasses on when it comes to romance and seeing how patiently and quietly you've loved me for years. So, I guess what I wanted to say was... that we should try this. Like, really give this thing a shot. We don't have to do anything drastic, and we definitely most likely shouldn't, because I want to give this the best chance of working that I can. So, if that's what you want, if you're willing to do this with me one step at a time, I'm going to be right there in step with you."

"Of course. God, of course. I love you. It just feels so good to say it. To finally be honest with you and with myself about it."

"I love you too, Beck Shepherd."

And then, I kiss her. I kiss her like I mean it, kiss her like I've wanted to every day since she's left. The salt from our tears mingles in our kiss, but it doesn't stop either of us — we've both been waiting for this. Wanting this. There's so much left to say, so much left for us to work out, and it takes all of my strength to pull away from her, but I know the last thing either of us need is to get carried away, so I do, giving her a grin as we laugh, our foreheads pressed together.

She smiles, and I don't think I've ever seen something so beautiful. All of the flowers in the world could not compare.

Chapter 24

Epilogue

Lydia

Six Months Later

As we sit together, watching Callie and Mason play with Amber and Melanie's daughter, Junie, I'm struck at first by how natural this one change had been.

I'd spent so much time being so afraid of it. Being so resistant to the way that life ebbs and flows, trying to dig my heels in and stop the world from turning. But if it had stopped, there would never be this little miracle running around in Amber and Melanie's new backyard. The January cold has us all chilled to the bone, sitting around by the fire pit and holding onto our hot chocolate for dear life, but Junie is completely unphased by it. She's four years old today. Her adoption was finalized just a few days ago, and she made sure to tell Amber that "her new mommies are the best present ever". Naturally, we all cried, and I haven't been able to get over how amazing this kid is since. I don't think I ever really will.

Change is a good thing. If there was never any change, there would be no Junie in our lives. I also wouldn't be living my dream of traveling full-time. That change was a more gradual one, and it started with me submitting some of my older journal entries to Practical Travel to test the waters. But, once I realized how fulfilled I was by it, I realized that I never wanted to do anything else. After I left my job at the firm, I was also able to start helping Beck sell some of his pottery on the side. Business is good, too — He's got a very successful Etsy page now, which is probably the cutest thing anyone has ever done, in my opinion.

"She's perfect," Beck says as he watches Junie chasing Mason with a Nerf gun, "I have the most perfect niece. Isn't she just the best?"

"Junie's pretty great, yeah," I agree, taking his hand in mine, "No kid will ever compare."

"Well, besides our own."

Our eyes meet, and my smile is instant. I probably shouldn't be surprised by this, probably shouldn't be surprised by how much I find that I've been expecting this, too, but I am all the same.

"You want to have kids with me?" I ask, because it's the only sentence my brain can form.

"Of course I do." Beck shrugs like it's not even a question, and his confidence in the matter grounds me. After standing on shaky ground with Tristan for so long, Beck is a breath of fresh air. Beck is a sure thing, my steadfast supporter and constant partner.

"When?"

"Probably after we've been married for a year or two. I want you all to myself for a while, you know."

This isn't the first time we've talked about marriage, even though it's the first time we've talked about having kids. Once I moved into Beck's house, we sat down and mapped out where this whole thing would be going. A careful plan for the future. Beck was very practical about it all, and his timeline would give me time to settle into my new career and feel secure while still allowing us some structure. We aren't engaged yet, but I know that it's coming, because Olivia (in the midst of my Maid of Honor duties for her) had gotten me to send her photos of rings that I liked. We also decided together that we didn't want anything extravagant, just a simple court-house wedding — we've both already done the whole big wedding thing, and we're perfectly content just to elope with a few of our closest friends and family.

"Well, naturally, I don't want to have kids right out of the gate," I tell him, "But my biological clock is ticking. You know that when women get pregnant after thirty-five, they call it a 'geriatric pregnancy', right?" I try to say this in a joking manner, but Beck looks at me in shock, and I laugh even harder at how appalled he looks.

"What the hell?" He asks me in genuine outrage, "Who thinks thirty-five-year-olds are geriatric?"

"It's not me that will be geriatric, it's my eggs. We only have so many. Not like men who can become dads when they're 70 like Mick Jagger."

"I feel like I have to have a stern talking to with the medical community now. Everyone knows you never call a woman old. Especially not when they're literally creating life. That's so messed up."

"You're telling me."

"I'm offended on behalf of women everywhere." He throws his hands up in defeat, and even though we're joking with each other, I know that he probably would be very genuinely outraged if I were to be.

"See? This is why I love you."

"Oh, really?" He deadpans, "All this time, I thought you just wanted me for my body."

"Ha ha." I pat the top of his hand reassuringly. For a moment, though, I look back at Junie. She's probably the best result of change that there's ever been, and I can't help but imagine how she'll get along with Beck and I's hypothetical child. "Seriously, though. If you do want to have a little while of just us before we're parents, where does that put us on the timeline?" Beck scratches the side of his face as he considers this. His beard is extra full now that it's winter, and he looks even more grown than he had before. He's so gorgeous, and he's all mine forever.

"Well," Beck says after a moment of consideration, "Uh, a year out from marriage, at most? I guess?"

"Hm." I muse, trying (and failing) to hide how obviously giddy that prospect makes me. "That's exciting. But I just..." I trail off, trying to search for the right words to say what I want to. "Well, nevermind."

"No, say it," Beck insists, turning his body to face me. "What are you thinking?"

"Well, isn't that just... another year of just us we could have? I know that we kind of do have it, because we live together now and all that, and we get to spend most of our time together, but we know we want to get married. Why wait?"

"Seriously?" He asks, beaming as he looks over at me.

"Seriously," I say with a smile, and he laughs softly, kissing the back of my hand gently.

"All of this from the person who wanted 'baby steps'."

"The baby steps have been taken," I say, trying my best to sound very practical, "And now the baby is in a full-on sprint, I guess."

"Lydia Michaelson, if I didn't know any better, I'd think you were asking me to marry you."

"Oh God, no," I cringe, laughing him off, "I would never be the one to propose. I'm all for it, if that's what women want to do with themselves, but the idea of putting myself out there like that makes me want to curl up in a ball and die."

"That's so dark."

"I'm completely serious."

"Well," Beck muses, "I guess I should be the one to propose to you then, right?" I nod sagely over at him, having to resist the urge to crawl in his lap and kiss him right then and there.

My smile does nothing but widen.

"That would be ideal, yes." It's so easy with him, the jokes and the banter, and I never want it to stop. Luckily, it never has to.

"Hm. That's definitely something for me to consider, then."

"It would be in your best interest for you to propose if you want to marry me, definitely."

"I'd just go ahead and do it now, you know, if I'd had more time to prepare. Or if I had the ring, or if it weren't Junie's day."

"Oh, trust me. After the flower thing, you've really got your work cut out for you with this proposal. You outdid yourself with that one."

We smile at each other, then, and he leans over and kisses me tenderly, like I'm the most precious thing he's ever seen. We still have most of the flowers from that day — the violets are in planters in the sunroom because we brought them in for the winter. I was able to preserve some of the wisteria, too, and have it framed and hanging over our bed.

The violets, though, I haven't touched. They stay in the planters, evolving with the seasons. They bloom, they grow, and then they fall dormant. The only evidence that they're still alive is the bit of green that stays year-round.

I like to think of how prevalent change is for the flowers when I start to worry. How even they don't remain stagnant in this life, how natural it is.

The flowers have changed. And just like them, I have changed.

Thank you for reading!

I hope you loved book two of the series. This one hit a little closer to home for me and holds a special place in my heart.

For more of the Hopeless series follow me for updates.

Instagram: @authorhannawaldon
TikTok: @authorhannawaldon

Acknowledgements

Thank you, Cam. I never would have finished this book without you pushing me to get it done.

Hopeless Series

Coffee, Codes, & Cliches
Beck & Call
Book three TBD

Printed in the USA
CPSIA information can be obtained
at www.ICGtesting.com
LVHW091507130924
790907LV00006B/103

9 798868 990243